what we broke

MARLEY VALENTINE

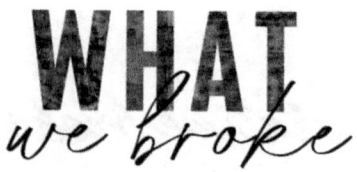

WHAT we broke

Cover design by Y'All That Graphic
Photographer: WANDER AGUIAR :: PHOTOGRAPHY
Model: Marcel
Edited by Shauna Stevenson at Ink Machine Editing
Edited by ellie McLove at My Brother's Editor
Proofreading by Jodi Prellwitz Duggan & Hawkeyes Proofing

This book contains mature content.

Andrew,
  you.
  you are my good days.

F.D. SOUL

author's note

What We Broke is a story about love and healing but also deals with some heavy topics. Please note that the following occurs on page:

- Stillbirth
- Passive Suicidal ideations
- Self-medication and alcoholism

While the main couple deals with their issues in the safety of a therapist's office and with a trained professional, this is still a fictional piece of writing.

If you ever find yourself in a situation where you need help, please do not hesitate to reach out to your national help hotline.

If you need any extra information on the subject matter in this book, please email the author at marleyvalentine@marleyvbooks.com

prologue

LEO

THERE WAS NOTHING BUT SILENCE.

For a room full of people, it was so hauntingly quiet.

Everyone spoke with their sad eyes and the hunch of their shoulders.

Nobody wanted to be here.

Not like this.

Not under these circumstances.

Rising up off my chair in the corner of the room, I walk out, purposefully keeping my head down to avoid looking at the way Jesse is sitting on the edge of the hospital bed, holding and comforting a distraught Zara.

Her skin is blotchy, cheeks red, eyes bloodshot, nose running. She's no longer crying. Her agonizing cries from before are now nothing more than soundless tears that won't stop falling.

I can't just sit here and watch as her body is poked and prodded and prepared to participate in something she didn't sign up for.

"Leo," Jesse calls out, but I don't stop.

With my hands fisted inside the pockets of my jacket, I

take myself to the small kitchenette located a few doors down.

Thankfully the room is empty, but as I try to shut the door on myself, Jesse's large frame slides into view, stopping me.

When Jesse's in a room, it's impossible to look anywhere else. Physically he's built larger than most. Between his height and the width of his shoulders, he easily takes up any doorway.

When God made him, He had surely sculpted him out of stone. He is a masterpiece that I have the privilege of admiring every day. His body is all toned muscles, deep lines, and perfectly placed dips. There isn't a day where I wouldn't beg to be held by this man, beg to be crushed under his strength and weight.

But Jesse's body has nothing on his face.

A face that had aged more in the last few hours than it had in all the seven years we've been together. There isn't one specific thing about Jesse Hunt's face that stands out. He has close-to-black hair, a thick but trimmed beard, and very common brown eyes.

But it's all about the details.

It's the way he looks at me with those eyes, the way they say, *"I want you. I need you. I love you."* The way each of his smiles says the words without him ever having to utter them.

It is life's greatest privilege to be in the presence of this man, to love this man and be loved by him.

Stepping farther inside, Jesse closes the door and reaches for me.

His large, calloused hands cradle my face.

Red rimmed and surrounded by thick, wet lashes, his

chocolate-colored eyes stare into mine, somber and over-flowing with sadness.

"What are you doing in here?" he asks, guiding me back until I'm pressed against a floor-to-ceiling cupboard.

Words fail me, so I shake my head, raise my hands in the air, and shrug.

His eyes brim with unshed tears and mine follow.

"I love you," he whispers, his voice soft, the emotion thick. "I love you so fucking much."

Gripping the collar of his shirt, I drag him to me, slamming my mouth onto his. But even with his lips on mine, a sob dislodges from my throat.

"Baby," he breathes out. "Tell me what you need."

The tears continue to fall and my body is now shaking, words still foreign.

Jesse releases the hold on my face and envelops me in his arms, hugging me to him tightly.

Closing my eyes, I continue to cry, and he starts kissing me, dropping soft pecks on the top of my head and my temple. I instinctively tilt my chin up and he slowly moves his mouth around my face. A kiss on each eye, kisses that line my jaw, kisses that catch my tears.

When our salty lips meet, we bask in the connection. It's not the type of kiss that leads anywhere, rather it's a kiss that keeps you grounded. In this moment, sharing the heartache and searching for strength.

When a tear that isn't mine lands on my upper lip, I know I'm not the only one overwhelmed with emotion. Pulling back, I open my eyes and see Jesse's own tear-streaked face.

It's exactly like him to abandon his own feelings and take on everybody else's; according to him there's no need for him to be the priority.

I run my thumbs across his cheeks, wiping away his tears, and press kisses to his face, like he did mine. "Tell me what you need."

It's his turn to reply with a hopeless shrug. "Yesterday we were painting and laughing, and today..." His words trail off with a swift shake of his head. "I don't know how we got here." He catches me off guard when he places a clenched fist over his mouth and tries to stifle a sob. "This wasn't supposed to happen," he cries. "Not to us. Not to you. Not to Zara."

"Hey," I soothe, dragging his fist away from his mouth and holding his face in my hands. "We'll figure it out," I assure him. "In time, we will figure this all out."

"I can't do this without you," he confesses before slamming his lips onto mine.

It's rough and unexpected but no less heartbreaking. His mouth ravages mine, the trepidation gone, but the desperation and sadness still the driving force. His hands curl around the length of my neck, his thumbs pressing painfully into my skin.

But I stay still and let him have at me, nothing more than a pliable participant, because if this is what he wants, he can have it. I will give him anything that helps with this debilitating loss we are both going to feel for years to come.

One hand travels down my body to find the hem of my shirt. Sliding his palm against my skin, he places it directly over my heart as his mouth continues to take.

"I'm sorry," he murmurs against my lips, hand pressing against my chest. "I'm so sorry. I know how much you wanted this."

"We," I correct, placing my own hand firmly over his and squeezing. "*We* wanted this."

He nods just before returning his lips to mine. We're

back to slow and measured, a little less take and a whole lot more give.

A knock startles us both, and we pull apart as the kitchenette door opens. Glancing over Jesse's shoulder, I see a familiar nurse's face, her sad smile telling me everything I need to know.

"We'll be there in a second," I inform her.

Nodding, she closes the door behind her, and I shift my eyes back to him and press my forehead to his. "Highs and lows," I say to him.

I watch his chest rise and fall as he repeats, "Highs and lows."

With his hand squeezing mine, we walk back toward the hospital room, and for a single moment, I think maybe we can survive this. Maybe everything will somehow be okay.

Unfortunately, that would become the very first lie I ever would tell myself about my marriage.

Stepping into the room feels like I'm climbing up a mountain, the altitude getting higher, the air getting thicker.

It's impossible to breathe.

I tighten my hand around Jesse's, certain I'm cutting off his blood supply as I take in the view in front of me.

Zara has been propped up with pillows, and the nurses are now maneuvering her hospital gown to expose her swollen belly.

I can't take my eyes off her stretched skin. Can't stop thinking about how many times I had casually touched Zara's stomach. Remembering all the times I knelt down on the ground to speak to our baby girl, and how hard she kicked when she heard my voice.

I can't breathe.

My head lifts and I meet Zara's watery, pain-filled, guilt-ridden gaze, and my next breath becomes even harder. There was so much history between us. So much love and friendship and happiness that felt unjustly strained right now.

We all had big feelings, and there was no handbook on how to navigate them in this situation.

"Okay, Zara. Leo and Jesse." Dr. Wong, our obstetrician breezes through the room, her voice reaching us before she does. She glances between the three of us and then keeps her eyes on Zara, who is noticeably in pain. "I'm glad you're all here. Zara, as I already told you, you're fully dilated and you mentioned pressure building, so we're going to reduce the amount and strength of your epidural and get ready to start pushing."

The doctor's voice softens as she adds, "I know this is not an ideal situation. So, please take the time to ask any questions or request any clarification. I will do my very best to make this as seamless as possible for the three of you."

"We appreciate that," Jesse answers.

"Now, do you both want to stand on either side of Zara?" It was less of a question and more of a statement. Because why wouldn't we? It had been the three of us from the very beginning, with a tighter bond than most.

I feel Jesse release his hold on me and I just stand there.

As he settles beside Zara, he looks up at me, expectantly. "What are you doing?"

"I want to be here," I state.

Confusion mars his face. "Zara needs us."

I shake my head just as Zara interjects, one hand cupping the bottom of her stomach and the other on Jesse's forearm. "Leave him. Let him do what he wants."

"Okay," Dr. Wong says. "It's time."

Focused on nothing else but what is coming, I'm rooted to the spot, and it has nothing to do with Zara and everything to do with an innate need to watch our daughter as she enters this world.

I want to be there every step of the way.

I want her to feel the same love we had for her when she was inside Zara's stomach, on the outside.

"I'm staying here," I say more forcefully.

This time nobody argues, but Jesse's gaze finally eases in understanding. Dr. Wong begins to settle herself between Zara's widened legs, and two labor and delivery nurses enter the room and begin to fuss over Zara, checking her blood pressure, timing contractions, and giving her instructions.

And I feel a part of me almost dissociate.

Voices sound like I'm underwater, and everything around me moves in slow motion, but I can acknowledge that time itself is moving forward.

Because I notice the shift in the room and see the change in Jesse and Zara.

Deep breaths. Long breaths. Pained breaths.

Exhaustion and sorrow behind every single push.

"She's coming." Dr. Wong's words seem to find me through my mental fog. "Just a few more pushes."

"I can't," Zara cries.

"You can," Jesse assures her. "You're doing amazing."

A final guttural sob leaves Zara's mouth, and my chest recognizes the pain as I watch Dr. Wong slide the small, delicate body from Zara's.

Reverently, she places our baby in the blanketed arms of one of the nurses, who walks her to me, caution in every step.

The tears fall, or maybe they never really stopped.

I hold my arms out, ready to cradle our bittersweet baby. She weighs no more than two and a half pounds, but the weight of our loss will crush me always.

"Hey there, sweet girl," I whisper. "Papa's got you."

I touch her small tuft of light-brown hair and circle the pad of my thumb over her soft cheek.

Bringing her closer to my face, I gently press my lips to the top of her head and inhale the scent of her.

"I love you so much," I choke out. "So, so much."

I feel Jesse sidle up behind me. His front presses to my back, his arms around my waist, his head looking down at her over my shoulder.

"She's beautiful." His voice trembles as he asks, "Same name?"

I nod.

"Hey, Lola girl," he whispers. "I'm your daddy."

The pain in his voice is unmissable.

Keeping my hold on her, I turn in his arms so she's resting between us. We both look down at her, the center of our world.

"She looks so peaceful," I tell him. "Here, hold her."

Careful not to jostle her, I place her in his waiting arms.

"She couldn't be more perfect."

He kisses her head and her cheek before glancing over his shoulder. And that's when I finally remember Zara.

My eyes follow Jesse as he walks our daughter over to Zara, and I'm no longer looking at Zara, my friend. Zara, our biggest supporter. Zara, who gave up so much of her own life to make our dreams come true.

No. As I watch Jesse hand Lola to Zara and sit beside her, comforting her, my brain doesn't remember that Zara.

My brain remembers Jesse's best friend, Zara. The

mother of Jesse's first daughter, Zara. Our egg donor, Zara. Our surrogate, Zara.

My brain insists on remembering Zara, the woman my husband should've married.

The woman who could live a whole, fulfilling life with Jesse, better than I ever can.

CHAPTER ONE

jesse

ONE YEAR LATER

FOR THE MILLIONTH TIME TONIGHT, I turn from my stomach to my back and reach out to the empty space beside me. I roll myself over to *his* side and bury my face in *his* pillow.

Inhaling, my senses search for his scent, my chest deflating and aching at just how little of it is left. A reminder that the distance between us widens as the smells of soap and sex and sleep are nowhere to be found.

"Dad?" The sound of my teenage daughter's voice at my bedroom door startles me.

"Yeah?" Throwing the blankets off in a hurry, I swing my legs over the side of the bed and reach for my sweat-pants. Frantically, I dart my eyes around the hard surfaces of my room, searching for my cell phone. "Why are you awake? What's the time?"

When I open the bedroom door, Raine stretches her arm out and hands me my cell. "You left it charging in the kitchen." I grab it off her and she adds, "There's a message you should read."

Frowning down at the screen, I see a text I wish Raine hadn't.

> GIO: I KNOW TODAY WAS HARD. HE ASKED ME
> TO PICK HIM UP AGAIN, BUT I'M NOT GOING. IT
> NEEDS TO BE YOU.

Raising my head, I meet my daughter's gaze. "Did you read this?"

Offering me a sad smile, she nods.

"Are you going to be okay alone?" I ask her.

"I could come with you."

A humorless laugh leaves my mouth. Somehow driving in the middle of the night to pick up her drunk dad isn't on the list of daughter and father activities I want to do together.

I lean in and kiss her forehead. "Please be asleep when I get back."

Walking back into my bedroom, I slip on a sweatshirt and thread my arms through my winter coat. Considering I was in bed only ten minutes ago, I'm sure I look ridiculous with all the layers. But it's cold out and I don't really know what to expect when I leave here, or how long I'll be gone.

Finding my boots, I shove my sock-covered feet in each one and head to the front door.

"Dad." My hand rests on the handle, the tone of my daughter's voice making it hard for me to turn around and face her. "Dad," she repeats firmly.

I attempt to swallow over the wedge of emotion stuck in the back of my throat and rest my head against the wooden door. "Yeah, babe."

"Is he okay?"

We both know the answer. Nothing has been okay in a very long time. But for her sake and mine, I lie anyway. "It's been a hard day, but everything is fine."

"That's not what I asked."

Get yourself a perceptive, mature seventeen-year-old daughter, they said. You'll love it, they said. What everyone forgot to prepare me for was the fact that this girl could read me like a book. There isn't a single thing that went unnoticed, and right now I *need* her to stop noticing.

I need her to be uninterested and unobservant and ignore the fact that one of her fathers was leaving the house in the middle of the night, to once again try and save our family.

But I'm not so lucky.

There is sadness and worry in her eyes, and I can't stand the disappointment and shattered expectations. She is my everything.

But so is he.

Together, they are my world.

The life we share is all I've ever needed, and then some.

But right now my heart is breaking right down the middle for all of us.

It's been a year and I'm in purgatory.

Raine is supposed to be applying for colleges. She's supposed to be getting ready to spread those wings and fly.

Our marriage was never supposed to be her problem. She doesn't need to be considering gap years, and I don't need her to make her life decisions based on the utter mess her parents have become.

But God how I want her here. Want her to stay.

She is the light at the end of a very dark tunnel.

The sun after a rainy, cloud-filled day.

She is the reason there is only one man getting drunk at a bar in the middle of the week and not two.

Her hand rests on my back, her comfort and empathy

emanating from that simple touch. It makes me want to drop to my knees and cry.

It wasn't supposed to be like this.

This isn't where I saw our life going.

"Here," she says quietly. "I packed you a few bottles of water, because he'll probably need them."

Attempting to find my resolve, I try to steady my shuddering breath and turn to face her. "Thank you." I grab the small cooler bag she's holding out for me and look at her pointedly. "*Please* be asleep when I get back."

"You know I can still hear you both when you get home, right?"

"Then just pretend for me, okay?"

Her knowing eyes find mine and she nods.

She knows what I'm asking of her. What I've *been* asking of her and what I will *continue* to ask of her.

Please turn a blind eye to the destruction of your parents' marriage.

Please let me live in denial.

Please, please, please let's just pretend.

Stepping closer, she rises up on the tips of her toes, kisses me on the cheek, and wraps her arms around my neck. "Goodnight, Dad."

Glad she's no longer going to argue with me, I exhale in relief and hug her around the waist, murmuring into her hair, "Goodnight, Raine."

Reluctantly releasing my hold on her, I watch her retreat to her bedroom and wait for the click of the door before leaving the house and climbing into the car.

The drive isn't as long as I need it to be.

It isn't long enough to quell the mishmash of feelings unfurling inside my chest. It isn't long enough to tune out the never-ending fight between my head and my heart.

Logic told me he was spiraling. *We* were spiraling. We had been all year. But my heart didn't care. My heart was his and had been since the moment I laid eyes on him. To have and to hold. To love and protect. But there were also the unspoken vows. Like how my heart was his to wreck and to ruin. To damage and destroy.

I was confident we were the forever type of love, even if right now we are nothing more than a hollow center and frayed edges.

Time isn't an issue, we could come back from this.

We would.

We had to.

Pulling into the parking lot, I find a spot as close to the entry as possible. Being a weeknight, there isn't much of a crowd; just a few suits dragging their feet before they call it a night.

Unable to pinpoint exactly how I'm feeling, I drop my forehead to the steering wheel and concentrate on my breathing.

One.

Hold.

Two.

Release.

I don't know what to expect when I walk inside. I'm used to the aftermath; the occasional lump of limbs curled up in our guest bedroom, the grunts that replace words, the hungover man who refuses to spend more than seconds around me and in our house. He wants to drown alone and I can't handle watching him do it—that is my reality.

This. This is the part we were both avoiding.

When the sound of muffled voices reaches my window, I raise my head just in time to watch a group of smiling men and women hug and kiss each other goodbye.

The simplicity of their moment makes me ache for the past.

Ache for a smile. A hug. A laugh.

Focused on the group of strangers, I almost miss the man with his head bowed, hands shoved deep into his jacket pockets, slinking unsteadily out of the bar.

He struggles with every second step, and after only a few, he gives up, resting his back against the brick building and sliding down to the pavement.

Looking lost and helpless, he closes his eyes and just sits there.

Alone.

It goes against every fiber in my being to watch him looking like that, but curiosity and anger keep me rooted to the seat.

Is this what he does when he's out? While I'm at home, alone with Raine, trying to be there for her, worrying about him and trying to maintain my own sanity; is this what he does?

Lately, I've been of two minds; full of both empathy and resentment toward this man. Because we have both loved and we have both lost, we are both hurt and broken, we are both sad and angry.

More nights than not, I too wanted to get lost in the bottom of a bottle. For a few single moments, I would love to forget that bad things happen and that we were victims to one of life's cruel jokes.

But as I acknowledge the shake in his shoulders as he sits on the cold sidewalk in the bitter night air, I would trade the bottle to be able to wrap him up in my arms. I would haul him onto my lap and let him bury his head in my neck as I tell him, over and over, everything will be okay.

Not today.

Not tomorrow.

But if he was by my side, I would make it okay. Eventually.

I would try.

For him I would.

For him I would move heaven and hell or die trying.

Movement in my periphery interrupts my thoughts, and my eyes dart over to see a man exiting the bar, looking left and right, searching for someone. My blood begins to simmer beneath my skin as I watch recognition and relief wash over his face before he walks toward my husband, plants his body beside him, and rests his hand on his knee.

Leo turns his head, and the familiarity that fills his eyes at the sight of this man, paralyzes me.

What the fuck?

My body is moving before my mind has a chance to talk me off the ledge. Climbing out of the car, I slam the door, and that causes enough of a disruption for both men to look up and notice me.

My gaze is trained on Leo, searching for guilt and suspicion. But all I'm met with is his usual vacant, desolate stare, and when that bothers me more than the possibility of my husband cheating, any sliver of hope I felt about us "working it out" disintegrates into dust.

When I finally reach them, I keep my eyes trained on Leo and speak to the stranger. "You can leave now."

Huffing, he reluctantly drops his hand off Leo's knee and stands up. "He needs water and food."

Clenching my jaw, I step closer to him. "How about you don't tell me what my husband needs."

He bites the inside of his cheek and glances down at Leo, who couldn't look more broken if he tried.

"You're right. Not my monkey, not my circus." He raises his eyes to meet mine and adds, "See you tomorrow, Leo."

Knowing he just threw a lit match on our already burning house, he smirks at me and retreats back inside.

It's on the tip of my tongue to ask who the fuck he is and how the fuck he knows our business, but when Leo tries and fails to stand up, my attention is diverted to *this* crisis.

I watch him stumble and fall again while slurring, "I didn't call you."

"No." I run a hand over my face before extending my arm out, waiting for him to take my hand. "It seems I'm the last person you would call."

Ignoring my attempt at assistance, he slumps his body back down on the concrete. "Why are you here?"

"Gio texted. He doesn't want to be the drunk man's taxi anymore."

"I'm not drunk," he argues. He finally manages to pull himself up off the ground and stand toe-to-toe with me, as if to prove his point. "And I'm not going home with you."

"Leo." I sigh. "Please."

I raise my hand to his cheek and he flinches. "Don't touch me."

His words lance through me, bringing home just how broken we are.

Once upon a time he couldn't get enough of my hands on him.

"Then get yourself in the car," I snap.

Ignoring me, he plucks his cell out of his pocket and starts tapping at the screen. He raises it to his ear. "I'm calling Gio."

Snatching it out of his fingers, I put it in my own pocket

and step forward. Taller and broader than him, I place both of my hands on either side of his face and cage him in.

He smells like a brewery, but it's still not enough to have me turn away or be turned off by him.

Out of habit, my eyes dart down to his mouth, and when his tongue peeks out to lick his bottom lip, I know he's not as immune to me as he insists on pretending to be.

Despite his continuous rejection, I take advantage of our close proximity and the fact he hasn't pushed me away. I give myself a reason to touch him and swipe some wayward strands of hair off his clammy forehead.

Holding his stare, I keep my voice steady and calm but firm. "You're coming home with me," I start. "We'll drive home together in our car and you'll sleep at our house, in our bed."

At the mention of us sharing a bed he squeezes his eyes shut and shakes his head, and my resolve crumbles at the sight.

"I won't touch you," I concede. "I'll even sleep on the couch."

"Jesse," he whispers. "Please. Stop."

"No," I bite out. "I need you to come home, Leo. Raine needs you to come home."

His eyes fly open, green orbs clashing with mine, and for the first time I see more than his sadness.

"Don't," he grits out. "Don't bring her up."

My eyes widen incredulously. "Don't bring up our daughter?"

"She's not—"

I slam my hand against the brick wall, the hard hit reverberating all the way up to my elbow. "She's not what, Leo?" I shout. "She's not what?"

He clamps his lips shut and turns his head away from me, hiding his eyes.

"I fucking dare you to say it," I seethe.

I don't miss the tear that falls down his cheek or the hiccupped sob that escapes his lips. I can't even stay mad at him when he's like this. And he *always* ends up like this.

Using the heels of his hands, he presses against his eyes and tries to stop his imminent breakdown. But between the alcohol and the fatigue, he slides down once more against the brick wall, landing with his knees pressed up to his chest. His arms wrapped around his legs, and his face buried in his lap.

I hate seeing him like this.

It makes me want to kick and scream and break things. I want to make something or someone hurt just as much as he is right now.

As the anger from earlier dissipates, I take a seat beside him. His head uncharacteristically drops to my shoulder and his body starts trembling.

He is so lost.

We both are.

Turning, I press my face into his hair and just breathe him in.

"I lost my job," he whispers.

I don't move a muscle at his confession.

I don't blink.

I don't breathe.

I don't break down.

We *need* his job. And he knows that.

Things have been tight for a while, and this is pouring salt into a wound that is already so deep, I'm certain it will never heal.

He is never going to let it.

"We'll be okay," I lie. "You'll find a new one."

Of that I have no doubt, but will he be able to start a new job and not let this black cloud of heartache follow him around? The answer is very unlikely.

He wants to self-sabotage.

I am certain he wants to kill himself without ever having to pull the trigger.

The only problem is, I want to go with him.

Because holding him up and trying to find reasons for him to be happy and present is exhausting. It's painful, and everything I try to sell him is a downright lie.

"Aren't you sick of being mister positive?" he scoffs as he moves out of my hold and rises to his feet. "We'll get through this," he mimics. "You'll find another one. We're going to be okay." His voice gets louder as he paces in front of me. "Aren't you fucking sick of it? Aren't you fucking sick of lying to us both?"

It's like he opened up my brain and took every single one of my thoughts and gave them life. What he's saying is exactly how I feel, but I don't give him the satisfaction of agreeing, staying silent as I jump to my feet.

Surprising me, he walks wordlessly toward my parked car, and I follow him. When he reaches the passenger side door he just stands there, staring out into the distance.

"I can't do this, Jesse." This time his voice loses the hysteria, sounding so cold and more detached with every word that follows. "It's been a year and I can't go back—to the way it was before. I thought it would get easier, but I can't do it."

Walking up behind him, I fight the urge to wrap my arms around his waist and stand close enough for him to know I'm right here.

"I haven't asked you to," I counter. "Besides begging

21

you to come home for the last six months, I haven't asked a single thing of you."

"Well, I can't do that either." He lets his head hang between his shoulders. "You know I can't. I can't be in that house with you. And Raine. And all the..."

All the memories.

All the plans.

All the things we wanted but no longer have.

"What are you asking of me, Leo? Are you really asking me to let you go?"

"Please," he breathes out.

This time I run the risk and press my front to his back, needing him to feel the weight of me and hear every single word that's about to leave my mouth.

"The only way I'll ever let you go is if I'm six feet under." I glide the tip of my nose down the length of his nape, enjoying the hitch in his breath and the way his body shivers against mine. "It's till death do us part, baby. And we're both still here."

CHAPTER TWO

leo

MY BODY ACHES. Everywhere.

My heart holds the most hurt, and most days it feels like the desecrated organ manifested pain into every bone and every muscle I have.

Mornings are the one moment when, for a fraction of a second, my day starts with a clean slate. When there is one single opportunity to inhale and exhale freely.

It is the one time I am free of the heavy and everything still has hope and possibilities.

It is also that one, same moment when realization hits and it all comes flooding back.

The memories, the agony, the torturous weight of sadness and loss.

That first reminder is paralyzing.

Every morning, lying in bed, staring at the off-white-colored ceiling, stiff and sore and so fucking hopeless.

There is a quiet knock on the bedroom door.

It's been eight weeks since the night at the bar. Eight weeks since Jesse begged me to come home. Eight weeks of

Jesse knocking at the same time every morning, and every morning I pretend to sleep through it.

Dragging the blanket up the length of my body, I pull it up over my shoulders and my head. It's no secret to either of us that I'm avoiding him. I'm avoiding the small talk over breakfast, and I'm avoiding any real effort at rejoining any routine that resembles our old life.

He knows that and I know that, but we're going through the motions anyway.

"Leo," he calls through the door. I imagine him close, his forehead pressed against the hollowed out wood. "Baby."

My eyes sting at the endearment, now turned into a hoarse, desperate plea. I hate how easily the words slip from his lips. How can I treat him like absolute trash and the man never wavers?

I hate that I'm not like him. That I can't just exist as his husband in the aftermath of it all.

Trying to ignore him, I bury myself deeper beneath the heavy blanket. It's what I'm good at, because while he's trying so hard to save us, I'm trying even harder to ruin us.

"Papa." My body stiffens at hearing Raine. She is my kryptonite and he knows that, but she's been avoiding me just as much as I've been avoiding her.

There is everything wrong with the way I've been acting toward her, but I'm struggling. I'm struggling to be present with the people who are here, living with me in the now.

I know she's hurting, but I don't know how to prioritize her pain over mine. I've lost the ability to be anything but self-centered, proving that maybe I'm really not fit to be a parent, and the universe just knew before I did.

"Raine," he says sternly. "You're supposed to be waiting for me in the car."

"Papa," she repeats. "I just want to talk to you."

She is exactly like her father. Persistent and hopeful and so fucking selfless. Like him, she believes she can be the one to get through to me.

"Papa," she says again, this time her voice wavering. "I'm waiting for you."

"Leo." Jesse's voice is stern. Gone is the man who was patiently waiting for me to come through. This is Jesse the father, and Jesse the father would break that door open and rip me out of bed if I don't answer his little girl.

Because that's what she is.

She isn't mine.

She is his.

Throwing the duvet off me, I swing my legs over the edge of the bed and rummage for a sweatshirt in my pile of dirty clothes. Covering up, I shake out my body and open the door.

My gaze lands on Raine first. Her eyes wide and smile unmissable, she glances up at her father, then back at me. "I knew you would open up for me. I've been telling Dad I should wake you up every day."

"Yeah, babe," Jesse says stiffly. "You were right."

Raine throws herself at me, and the surprise almost causes me to lose my balance. Her arms squeeze around my neck, and as if I'm sitting in front of a warm fire on a winter's night, my shoulders soften, and the tension in my chest loosens.

As I hug her to me, my eyes find Jesse, who is staring at me, his own eyes filled with nothing but turmoil. I will myself to look away, but the man has always held me hostage.

We aren't just bound together by marriage vows, we are

tethered. Like magnets, my soul couldn't detach itself from his no matter how hard I tried.

And I'm fucking trying.

Raine releases her hold on me, still smiling. "I'll meet you in the car, Dad."

We watch her walk out of sight, leaving us to stand in silence.

It's suffocating, filled with all the things I know he wants to say and all the things I don't want to hear.

"We have that appointment this afternoon," Jesse says as I turn to retreat to my room.

"I know," I reply without looking at him. "I haven't forgotten."

I feel Jesse's hesitation seconds before I hear it in his voice. "I guess I'll see you later, then."

I know it isn't what he wanted to say to me, but we don't have much to say to each other anymore.

I listen for the sound of his footsteps retreating and the front door closing as I walk back into my own room. When the familiar snick of the lock echoes through the house, I release a loud exhale and let my body fall onto the bed.

Like clockwork, my phone vibrates on my bedside table and I groan into the mattress.

They're a tag team, refusing me a single moment of peace.

Reaching for it, I slide my thumb across the screen, answering the call and putting it on loudspeaker. "What?"

"Is that any way to greet your best friend?"

"Good thing you're not my best friend," I say flatly.

"And yet you keep answering my calls."

"Because you won't leave me the fuck alone."

For all intents and purposes Gio is my best friend, but the truth is, he's more than that. He's my brother. My only family. The only person who has been there for every high and low in my life. And despite our constant arguing lately, I need him. I just don't want to admit it to him.

"Seriously, though." His voice loses the humor. "How are you?"

It's a simple question that I have no answer for. There's not a single word that can encompass the tumultuous number of feelings that pass through me on a daily basis.

I am the seven stages of grief personified, but sometimes I don't know what I'm grieving the most: my past or my future.

The loss of what we had left a crater-sized hole in our hearts, lives, and my marriage, but the loss of what we could've been feels insurmountable.

Like no version of the days ahead would do.

It's the reason I want to drink every night and sleep through every day. I'm rooted in purgatory, unable to work out what's supposed to happen next.

"Leo," Gio says. "Talk to me."

I let my silence answer him.

"You have your session with Jesse today, right?" he continues, tempting me to respond. "Are you looking forward to it?"

I scoff. "Looking forward to it? He won't give me a divorce until we attend couples' counseling; it's a fucking bribe. Don't try to build this up into something it's not."

"You love him," he states. "Working on your marriage is the right thing to do."

"Right thing for who?" I snap.

I hear his impatient breath through the phone. "You love him, Leo. This is stupid."

"You're supposed to be on my side."

"I am," he counters. "But I can't just sit by and let you make the biggest mistake of your life."

I ignore his concerns, because they aren't my concerns and they aren't valid. I need this divorce. I need away from Jesse. Away from the reminder of everything we lost. Away from this life he thinks we can have.

"Just let it go, Gio. This is none of your business anyway," I spit out. "Isn't that why you sided with him and kicked me out of your house? Agreed with him that I should go home, huh?"

"Fuck you," he growls. "I let you stay with me for six months. Six fucking months of you barely making it to work. Six fucking months of you hiding out." He catches his breath before continuing. "And my house is yours, always, Leo. But you have a husband and a daughter waiting for you every night in that big, beautiful, this-is-what-dreams-are-made-of house of yours, and you insist on fucking burning it all to the ground. And for what?" He lowers his voice, calming down, hoping to help me find reason. "I know you're hurting, but so are they. Hurt and heal with your family, Leo."

"Like I said," I say emotionlessly. "It's a bribe. Jesse and I are done."

"Mr. Ricci-Hunt," the receptionist calls out. "Dr. Sosa says you can go on in."

I glance around the empty waiting area. Jesse's unusually late, and discomfort takes root in my stomach.

"I'm waiting for my..." I stall at calling him my husband, and the lady behind the desk offers me a sad smile. Obviously aware of why people attend her office.

"Your husband," she finishes for me "That's fine. Dr. Sosa is happy to start without him."

Feeling unsettled, I make my way through to our therapist's office.

Dr. Sosa is a woman closer to my age than I'd like her to be. In her mid-thirties, with her pencil skirt, and short, brown-haired bob, she seems so put together, it makes old inadequacies creep to the surface.

It's not her intention to make me feel this way. In fact, if I had chosen a therapist myself, it would've been her. But old wounds never really heal, and I haven't felt this insecure and uncertain of myself in such a long time.

"Hey, Leo," she greets, a wide smile on her face. "It's so great to see you again."

Nodding, I take a seat on the single chair. "Uh, Jesse doesn't seem to be here yet."

"Yes," she confirms, taking a seat and rearranging a leather folder on her lap. "He called and said he would be a little late."

"Oh. Okay." I try to school my features, hiding the unwarranted irritation that surges at the thought of him choosing to tell our therapist instead of me.

"Plus," she starts, "you and Jesse gave consent when it comes to either of you talking to me without the other present."

My back shoots ramrod straight. Consent or not, I did not sign up for this.

"I don't have anything to say," I tell her. "Jesse is the one who wants us to be here."

"But you're the one who wants the divorce," she counters.

I grind my teeth, hating the ambush.

"This is your third session and you've yet to say

anything about why you want a divorce," she says. "You've yet to say anything about anything, really, and I would've thought you'd be here with an argument ready."

She's probing, trying to bait me, but I'm not going to bite. I've had plenty of practice with Jesse. Plenty of practice avoiding the truth and keeping the pain to myself.

As far as I was concerned, the one reason I did have was enough. "We lost our baby," I say flatly, despite the agony that rips through my heart at the mere mention of Lola. "I don't want to move forward. I don't want to pretend we're okay. I don't want to do anything else besides miss my baby girl."

My eyes fill with unshed tears and my throat tightens, the emotion thick and suffocating, but I remain still, my gaze on Dr. Sosa's, refusing to give even an extra ounce of information.

"But I haven't asked you to do any of those things." Jesse's voice is soft and gentle, a tone I haven't earned nor do I deserve.

I look over my shoulder, the sight of him in oil-stained jeans and a hoodie has the blood flowing beneath my veins rising to simmer, but it's the broken look on his face that cools me right down.

I put that there. And I continue to put that there, and I don't know how to stop.

I'm not purposefully trying to hurt him.

I don't want the divorce because he's a bad husband and I've fallen out of love with him. It's actually the complete opposite.

I love him. So much it fucking hurts.

I will never love anyone the way I love this man, but it doesn't fix the soul-shattering pain our daughter's death brought about.

The simplicity of it all is that I can't come back from it.

I don't know how, or I don't want to, I'm not completely sure. But I know it is absolutely unfair to keep a man as wonderful as Jesse Hunt plastered to my side in the hopes that the old me will return.

Jesse walks into the room, the space feeling smaller almost immediately. He sits on the sofa beside me, eyes dancing around my face. "I wanted you home, Leo. I wanted you grieving, *with me,* at home."

We haven't done a lot of talking since Lola died. Unless alcohol was involved, we converse through other people and with others around. This is as private and direct as we are ever going to get, and he is waiting for me. Expectantly waiting for an explanation I can't give him.

"I'm home," I argue.

"Home," he scoffs. "It hasn't been home to you since Lola died. Six months later you left with a bag to go to Gio's house and just never came back. Now you're out there pretending to look for work or drinking just enough to be able to bring yourself home every night. And on the odd night where you decide to stay in, you're holed up in your room, because you want a divorce and I gave you an ultimatum," he snaps, the veins in his neck protruding the angrier he gets. "Not because you want to be there."

Between Jesse and Gio, there was not a single lie told, and silence is my only defense.

"Really?" He runs his hands over his now red face. "I can't believe you've got nothing to say."

I glance at Dr. Sosa, expecting her to step in, but she doesn't. There's no more kid gloves and dancing around the obvious in this week's session—she's happy being here and watching me drown.

I should've expected it to come to a head at some point,

because this is Jesse after all. He's not known for his patience. And the fact that he has stood by for *months* while I've drunk myself stupid and hidden from him at Gio's house isn't lost on me.

I've taken the disruption to our life and I've run with it. And unlike the man who would not take no for an answer when I didn't want to date him, this Jesse is giving me space, giving me time, allowing me to grieve.

It was the right thing for him to do, despite it being against his nature to do so, and I don't know if I love or hate him for it.

Jesus, I am such a fucking mess.

This is the problem. I can't decide how I feel or what I want, and I'm taking Jesse on a fucking ride because of it.

For his sake and mine, I need him to let me go.

"I don't know what you want from me," I say truthfully. "I've told you it's all too much for me. I can't pretend to move on."

"Who the fuck has moved on?" he bellows, and my whole body flinches.

It was a shitty thing to say, but it's my truth. Our grief does not feel the same and it changed everything for me.

Jesse rises up from his seat in frustration and walks to the opposite end of the office, pacing the length of the room.

"I don't know what we're doing here," he says, looking at Dr. Sosa, voice full of defeat. "Isn't it supposed to get better?"

Slowly, she uncrosses her legs and places her notebook on the small table that sits in the middle of the room.

"Okay," Dr. Sosa interrupts. "Let's just take a minute before this gets too heated. I need you both to know that making the decision to come to therapy is a huge step for your relationship," she praises. "While I can tell it's difficult, it's not unusual for my couples to want different outcomes and have differing feelings." She darts her eyes between us. "Because of this I encourage both of you to commit to a period of time in therapy and we can potentially make some loose plans of what to do, depending on the outcome."

I can't help but shift my gaze to Jesse and find him already looking at me. There's no hiding the hurt and desperation in his eyes, the urgent need for me to change my mind.

"I'm not saying it's impossible to find common ground, but it should be noted we like to plan for when we don't," she says calmly. "I've noticed we're up to our third session and disclosing anything beneath the surface has been really hard, for both of you. I am concerned about how we can move forward without either of you really being heard or seen."

Jesse and I stare at one another, my heart squeezing at her honesty. I want the dissolution of our marriage, but it only just dawns on me that I'm going to have to destroy Jesse in the process.

"You're going to need to go right back to the beginning," she adds.

Without acknowledging her request, Jesse's eyes bore into mine, his thoughts clear. "The beginning was never the problem."

CHAPTER THREE

jesse

THEN

"JESSE," my best friend, Zara, sing songs. Seated in a booth, she slides herself across the faux leather seat closer to me and wraps an arm around my neck before kissing my cheek. "Don't look so fucking miserable, we're here to have a good time."

"I know how to have a good time," I tell her. "At home. In my bed."

"But why settle for your hand when you could have this." She waves her arm out, gesturing at the overcrowded bar. "Look at the plethora of men and women right at your fingertips."

My eyes scan the room, taking in the mixed crowd. It was the time of night when the businessmen and women were finishing up their last drinks and the partygoers were ready to let loose and start their weekend. I didn't fit in either box, but it was Zara's birthday and we had a whole history of birthdays we'd spent together. I wasn't about to break our tradition now.

"You know I'm not into any of this," I remind her.

"I know, I know. You're just here for me," she states. "You're a homebody, a marriage and kids type of man."

"I already have a kid."

"*We* have a kid," she corrects. "Pity marriage just wasn't in the cards for us."

"It is a pity. Think of how great your life would be if you were married to me." I reach for the tumbler of whisky in front of me. "We could be at home right now, drinking wine, ordering takeout."

Her shoulders rise to her ears and she makes an exaggerated retching sound. "No, thanks."

I nudge her in the stomach. "Shut your mouth. I would be a great husband."

"I'm sure you would be. But you're a terrible lay."

"What the fuck?" Placing my drink back down on the table, I turn my whole body to face her. "We were sixteen."

"And you got me pregnant," she adds.

"Which is irrelevant to this conversation," I counter. "I will have you know, now that I am not an eager, hormone-fueled teenager desperate to lose his virginity, nobody, and I mean *nobody*, has complained about my skills in the bedroom."

"Why do you think I never came back for seconds?"

"You never came back for seconds because, and I quote, 'nobody told you losing your virginity hurt worse than waxing your legs.'"

"Well, they didn't." She huffs. "Those girls, who were supposed to be my friends, bragging about how much they loved it? They fucking lied. Just you wait till our daughter is old enough to know the truth. There's no way I'll lie to her."

The thought of our daughter, Raine, being old enough to talk about sex has me reaching for my drink and emptying the contents in one sip. I wait for the burn to subside before speaking. "Can we not unnecessarily age our ten-year-old daughter and return to you amending your previous comment?"

"Amending it to what?"

I shrug. "I don't know, maybe something like 'he's great in bed, but I'm into women now.'"

"Yeah." She smiles mischievously. "I'm into women now because you were such a terrible lay."

We'd been friends since middle school and tried to have a go at being something more during our freshman year, only to find out we were not physically compatible. Kissing was weird, and after the fumbled night of sex where we both lost our virginity, anything more was a hard no.

Throw in an accidental teenage pregnancy, Zara coming out as lesbian, and me coming out as bisexual, and between us we've shared a *lifetime* of milestones.

But now we're in the smooth part of our lives. We have a solid foundation when it comes to both our friendship and our roles as co-parents. The platonic and familial love we share makes life effortless. It's the best case scenario when it comes to our "situation" and it's one I also know is both a rarity and a privilege.

"I fucking hate you."

She winks and blows me an exaggerated kiss. "Not even close, baby."

"Zara!" a chorus of voices shouts, interrupting our conversation. We both look across the table and catch a group of her friends pushing through the growing crowd of people and dancing to the music toward us.

Zara slaps a hand on my thigh. "I'm going to go meet them on the dance floor and save you from having to engage in any conversation."

Throwing an arm around her neck, I squash her to me,

planting an exaggerated kiss on her temple and then pushing her out of the booth. "Go. Have fun."

Laughing, she slides herself out and heads over to her friends.

I keep them in my line of sight, until flailing hands and arms catch my attention.

My gaze follows the interruption, landing on a slender man dressed in a baby blue, collarless linen shirt, tucked neatly into his white chinos. The first three buttons are undone, showing off a gold chain that sits gracefully against his smooth-looking chest and making my mouth water.

He is beautiful.

His sleeves are rolled up to his elbows and his three-quarter-length pants stop right at his ankles. With his bronzed skin and light-brown curls that fall into his face, he looks like he should've been on a million-dollar yacht, basking in the Mediterranean sun.

He's also the worst dancer I've ever laid eyes on, but Jesus Fucking Christ is he beautiful.

His tall, lean body jars and jolts awkwardly with every deafening beat of the music. And even uncoordinated and out of sync as he is, I can't take my eyes off him.

Following his every movement, my gaze travels from the tips of his fingers, down to the shoes on his feet. Taking inventory of the way this attractive, well-dressed, yet heavy-footed, man looks so perfect and at ease in his own skin. His carefree smile lights up his whole face, the lines at the corners of his eyes make him look well lived. Well loved.

I can't remember the last time I saw someone looking so happy. It makes me want to be close to him. I want to know all the reasons his smile is so big.

Amidst his crazy dancing, the beautiful stranger loses his footing, and another man's arms grab him around the waist, steadying him, and an unwarranted twinge of jealousy coils tightly inside my stomach.

It's ridiculous. I don't know him and he doesn't even know I exist.

I watch the two men interact, trying to work out if they are lovers or just friends. They are definitely familiar with one another and comfortable in each other's presence, but there isn't anything that gives me a definitive answer.

Both men are the same height. If I needed to guess, I would say they're just under six feet, which is shorter than my six foot three. And as the music changes to something less poppy and more seductive, the men gravitate toward one another and start to sway, sensually, to the different beat.

My new infatuation turns in his friend's arms so his back is resting on the other man's front. He's no longer the laughing, gangly-armed, dancing man.

The music shifts the mood, the air thick with sex and tension as the dance floor overflows with bodies grinding up on each other.

They're too close now, his friend gripping his hips tightly and rolling into him.

I try to drag my eyes away, leaving them be, but when his eyes lock with mine, all bets are off.

I wait to see if he holds my stare, hoping that even with another man's hands on him, it isn't at all what it looks like.

They continue to dance together, but when his gaze remains on my face and the side of his mouth tips up in almost a smirk, I decide I really don't care who he's here with.

Too enamored to worry about anyone or anything else around me, I stand, making my way out of the corner booth where I'm seated. I don't miss the way his eyes follow me, hungrily tracking the length of my body.

If I didn't have confirmation before, I have it now.

He's interested.

Playing it cool, I decide to get a drink, but I keep him in my line of sight. Finding a small opening, I squeeze my body between two groups of people and rest my forearm atop the marble bar.

I have the perfect view.

Arousal courses through every part of me, but despite how badly I want my hands to be on him, I wait patiently for the right moment to pounce. His smile is mischievous as he turns and links his arms around his friend's neck. His friend, oblivious to it all, bends his head and buries his face in his neck.

A rush of hot jealousy passes through me as his hands roam down the back of my mystery man and land on his tight ass and subtly squeeze. When mystery man pushes himself away from his friend, I decide I'm not waiting any longer.

Electricity thrums in my veins with every step I take.

With his back to me, he has no idea I'm coming, but his friend is watching me, looking puzzled and unsure. I should be slightly more concerned with how this will end up. He could be completely unavailable and I could just be inserting myself into a mountain of drama I don't need.

But for some inexplicable reason, I don't care.

Everything about this goes against all my rules.

I don't go out, and I don't pick up anyone at bars.

I don't do one night stands, but holy fuck do I want him.

And I *always* get what I want.

As if his body senses mine, he turns to face me, just as I approach them. Up close, his eyes are the color of the ocean, a beautiful combination of blue and green that only accentuates the sun-kissed color of his skin.

Instead of being surprised to see me, he steps away from his friend, who desperately tries and fails to keep his hands on him, and moves toward me.

My eyes dart to the man behind him and I take in the defeated look on his face. Whatever tonight was, it's obvious he'd hoped for more, and it's even more obvious he isn't getting it.

Prompted by our closeness, my body moves of its own accord. Like it's already done this before, my hands find their way to his hips and I bring him flush to me.

Looking up at me with wide eyes, he's surprised by my forwardness but not put off. This close, our differences are obvious. Where he looks like a perfectly carved-out sculpture, I am nothing more than a brute of a man in comparison. But, still, he doesn't put any space between us.

I lower my mouth to his ear, making sure he can hear me above the music. "Tell your friend you're done for the night."

He rears his head back and raises an eyebrow at me as if to say "is that so?"

"Don't act surprised," I say loudly, squeezing his hips. "I saw you watching me."

"You mean, you were watching me," he counters.

"And that."

He turns to look at his friend, who is now standing at the bar alone, looking like someone kicked his puppy, and then back at me. He raises his mouth to my ear. "I'm here with someone."

Standing like this, we look like a couple. Two men huddled together, close and cozy as we continue to try and talk despite the music. "And now you're leaving with someone else."

I can feel him shake his head. "I don't know anything about you."

My hand curls around the back of his neck, and I press a small kiss to the curve of his jaw. I feel a shiver race down his spine, and my cock thickens in response. "So, leave with me and get to know me."

"Just like that, huh?"

I shrug and he raises his wrist, checking the time on his watch before looking over his shoulder at his friend. "Meet me outside in ten minutes."

"I could say goodbye to him for you if you want," I tease.

Grinning, he pushes my hands away from his hips and begins to walk backward. He raises both his hands to show the number ten and then places them together, mouthing the word "please."

Remembering I'm also here with some people, I drag my cell out of my pocket and send Zara a quick text. She'll be too busy dancing and flirting to reply.

Putting my phone away, I head back to the booth to retrieve my jacket, giving him the ten minutes he asked for. Plus, I don't want to watch his friend make sad eyes at him when he tells him he's leaving.

I'm not a complete ass; I would hate to miss out on a night with him too.

Exiting the club, my eyes automatically land on that man who's watching me; waiting for me. I don't know how he managed to leave without me noticing, but with his arms crossed, leaning on a street pole, he looks even more stunning in the light.

Holding his stare, I push through the few people who are milling around the exit and close the gap between us. He rakes his teeth over his bottom lip the closer I get, his blue-green eyes bright and focused on only me.

I could get used to being the center of his attention.

"Hey," I say, extending my hand out to him. "I'm Jesse."

He looks at my hand for a beat too long, and I worry he might not take it.

"Leo." He slowly places his hand in mine. "What's with the formality? You didn't have a problem touching me without introducing yourself inside."

He's right. In the muted light of the club, I wanted nothing more than to touch him. I still want that. But under the bright street lights, I'm a long-game type of man.

And the game starts now.

Remembering he wears a watch, I tip my chin up at him. "What's the time?"

Despite the raise in his eyebrow at my question, he looks down and then back up at me. "Ten thirty."

"Are you hungry?" I ask.

Eyeing me curiously, he takes his hand out of mine and shoves both into the pockets of his chinos. His stance is casual and unbothered, but the words out of his mouth feel more like a test than a truth. "You don't have to feed me to fuck me."

Mirroring his own actions, I bury my hands in my own pockets and give him honesty. "Can't I do both?"

The way he rocks on his heels and attempts to hide his smile and fails lets me know whatever it is he was testing me on, I passed. "I guess the night is still young."

Moving us away from the club, I step away from him

and point in the direction of a twenty-four-hour diner that's only a few blocks up the road. "There's a place not far from here, if you're okay with me choosing."

He waves his hand in front of him. "Lead the way."

Together, we maneuver through the groups of clubgoers. When the crowd is finally behind us and it's only me and him and a few other people also walking toward the diner, Leo asks, "Do you come here often?"

I don't know if he means to the club or the diner, but either way, I don't miss the curiosity in his voice. And because I've already worked out that every question Leo asks me has a reason beyond curiosity behind it, I decide to toy with him a little.

"I do," I say with a straight face. "Every weekend. Troll the club, hit the diner, take home some ass, and come back next weekend and do it all again."

He stops mid-step, and I school my face before looking over my shoulder at him. "What?"

Chuckling, he continues to walk. "You've never picked anyone up in a club before, have you?"

Now side by side, we continue on, every one of his steps matching every one of mine.

"Not even once," I answer honestly. "Most nights you can't even get me to stay up past nine o'clock."

"And tonight?"

"Tonight I came out for my best friend's birthday and hated every minute until my eyes landed on this guy and his horrible dancing."

"I really am the worst dancer," he agrees.

"So, so bad." We both laugh, and it's an easy laugh, easy conversation. "Entertaining to watch, though. I like a man who's comfortable in his own skin."

"You don't have to compliment me, I'm already here with you."

Something about the way he keeps saying that I don't need to do or say anything "extra" because he's already agreed to leave with me, makes me feel uncomfortable.

It's obvious I'm missing something, but instead of addressing it, I ignore it.

"What about you?" I ask, changing the subject. "Regular at the club?"

"Is that your way of asking me if I sleep around?"

"I couldn't give a shit if you sleep around," I say truthfully. "I was just starting a conversation."

"Sorry," he says, guilt tingeing his apology. "This is all a bit new to me. I'm a little out of my element here."

I narrow my eyes at him just as we reach the diner.

"This," he says, pointing to the twenty-four-hour grease bowl. "Usually I'm already in the back of a cab and I've got some guy's hands on the back of my head as I clumsily take him down my throat. This," he repeats. "Is nothing like that."

While the image of me and him in the back seat of a car and his face in between my legs is enough to make my usually neglected dick stir to life, I know I don't want our night to go exactly like all those others.

When I asked Leo to leave the club with me, I didn't have a single thought past wanting to be near him.

I'm attracted to him, caught up in whatever it is about him that made me go against all my rules. And as he continues to unknowingly drop clues about himself, I'm even more certain bringing him to the diner first was the right decision.

There is no denying that, just like every man before me, I want him in my bed. But I know the quicker that time comes around, the closer I am to ending the night. He is a one-and-done man, and everything inside me is telling me this is more than that.

Wordlessly, I reach for the door and open it, gesturing for him to go inside.

He leads us to the back of the diner, sitting at a small two-seater table that would barely fit two plates of food on it if we were both eating.

As soon as I lower myself to the chair, a server appears out of thin air, a young woman who can't be older than twenty-one, yawning as she places two large menus the size of my head in the middle of the table.

Leo grabs them, and I watch his eyes do a quick perusal before passing them over to me.

"Do you know what you want?" I ask, dragging the laminated cardboard out of his hands and glancing down to choose from the list of items. It's very basic, and for that I'm grateful because I have a terrible time choosing only one thing to eat. "I think I'll just have—"

The server returns just as Leo plucks the menus back out of my hand and gives them to her. "We'll have the whole breakfast menu and two Cokes."

Choosing not to bring any attention to the fact that he said "we'll have" instead of "I'll have," I lift a finger in the air signaling the server to wait a second. "Could I please change that to a Dr. Pepper and a Coke, please?"

"Please tell me you did not just say Dr. Pepper." He groans.

"What's wrong with Dr. Pepper?"

"Everything." He covers his face with his hands and shakes his head. "It tastes like sugar and cough medicine."

"I happen to really like sugar and cough medicine."

"So that's one of each item from the breakfast menu?"

the server interrupts, reminding us she's still here and waiting. "And a Coke and a Dr. Pepper."

"Yes, thank you," I say.

She retreats to the kitchen, leaving us alone, and I trail my eyes over yet another version of my mystery man. The light in the diner is harsh and unflattering, but somehow he's even more gorgeous every time I look at him.

My eyes meet his, and I watch his Adam's apple bob in his throat. "Don't," he says.

At first I don't think I hear him correctly, because his request doesn't make sense, but when he averts his gaze I press the issue. "Don't what?"

When he was dancing in the club he looked so carefree and untroubled, but the man sitting across from me is different. He's reserved and a little unsure, and I want to know why.

"Look at me."

"It's kinda hard not to," I admit. "From the second I saw you in the club, it's been hard to do anything else but look at you."

It was slight, the flush that traveled up his neck and bloomed on his cheeks, but I caught it.

"Do you have to look at me like *that*, though?"

Utterly confused, I rest my forearms on the table and lean in, bridging the already small space between us. I watch Leo's demeanor change, his blue-green eyes devoid of their spark, as a new, shy and apprehensive version of my mystery man makes its first appearance.

"Look at you like what?" I ask cautiously.

He huffs. "Like you want to do something stupid."

I wait him out and he continues.

"Like you want to do something stupid and get to know me."

47

CHAPTER FOUR

leo

THEN

THIS WASN'T how the night was supposed to go.

The man in front of me is sex personified and he wants to feed me before he fucks me.

It's unexpected and completely unnecessary.

I spent so much time making sure that men only want me for my body, that his insistence makes me feel off balance.

My confidence is wavering, feeling myself being reduced to a quieter, more reserved version of myself who is basking in how much attention this man is giving me.

It isn't the obvious type of attention either, not like the way his eyes ate me up at the club, full of heat and greed. This is more muted, his attention focused on the things I keep close to my chest. Fixated on the things I don't say.

His eyes are currently zeroed in on me and I know this man is not about to let a single thing go.

"What's the big deal?" he asks. "What's wrong with me getting to know you?"

My tongue wants to form the words, more than they

ever have before—*I'm not worth it*— but instead I give him a half-hearted shrug. "The best thing about me is my body."

It's my default response, my shield, and very much the truth.

I watch him bite the inside of his cheek as he makes an exaggerated effort to tilt his head and drag his eyes up and down my body. "It's a great body," he says. "I'm sure it's even better without all your clothes on. But I find it hard to believe it's the *very best* thing about you."

"We could just go to your place or mine and find out."

He just keeps his eyes on me, his silence his answer.

"You're not going to let it go, are you?" I add.

He shakes his head. "I always get what I want."

I make an unidentifiable noise, something akin to a half chuckle, half huff. "You're really cocky, you know that?"

He shrugs nonchalantly. "It works."

It does, and that's what scares me. A little bit of extra attention from a man and I'm all twisted up. I'm sitting in a twenty-four-hour diner, telling a stranger that all I can offer him is my body while ordering enough food to keep us here for the whole night.

I'm nothing but full of contradictions.

"Listen." I swallow hard and look at him pointedly, not sure which one of us I'm trying to convince.

Surprising me, he places a hand over mine, and that immediately renders me speechless.

I slide my hand out from under his. "What are you doing?"

"Stop overthinking this," he soothes.

Before I have a chance to argue, the server returns, holding a large tray full of food high above her head. One at a time, she arranges the plates on the table.

Pancakes, eggs, bacon, crispy hash browns, chicken and waffles, French toast, and two empty plates.

I wait for a reaction from Jesse, but all he does is hand me some cutlery and a plate. When I ordered, I subconsciously may have hoped that ordering all this food would turn him off, but he doesn't seem the least bit fazed.

Lastly, she puts our drinks in the middle of the table and drops down the bill. I guess with free refills and the whole breakfast menu in front of us, it's a safe assumption that we won't be ordering any more or leaving anytime soon.

We'll be lucky if we even finish the food.

Grabbing his cutlery, Jesse cuts into the pancakes and serves himself a triple-stacked slice. He then proceeds to take a portion of every dish, creating a pile of mismatched food in front of him.

It's both gross and somewhat endearing.

"Are you really going to eat all that?" I ask.

He stops the fork full of food mid-air. "Isn't that why you ordered it?"

"So... what?" I ask stupidly. "We just sit here and eat and talk?"

He shoves a heap of crispy hash browns into his mouth and nods.

He continues to eat, tasting everything all at once, taking a sip of his drink after every bite, and I continue to watch. I'm completely out of my element yet one hundred percent entranced by this man.

Shaking my head, I grab my fork and knife and cut myself some French toast. Jesse eyes me as soon as I put some into my mouth, and as soon as the square of bread touches my tongue, I know why.

It's cold and soggy, and the overpowering taste of egg

makes it impossible to swallow. I search for a napkin and quickly bring the tissue up to my mouth, spitting the bread into it.

Jesse smugly hands me my drink and I take a long suck out of the straw, the fizzy liquid making my nose sting.

"What the fuck was that?" I breathe out, pushing the drink away from me. "You knew the whole time," I accuse. "But you just kept on eating."

Still smirking, he wordlessly puts some bacon in his mouth. And for some ridiculous reason, I follow suit, tasting nothing but salt and regretting it instantly.

"Jesus." I take another sip out of my straw and lean over the table, snatching Jesse's fork out of his hand. "It's horrible. Stop it."

"It's not that bad," he counters, trying to take back the cutlery.

"Are you crazy? Stop eating it. We can go find something else," I ramble.

He stills. "We can?"

"We can what?"

"Find somewhere else to eat?"

It takes a few seconds for my brain to realize what I've said and what Jesse is asking. I shake my head from side to side. "You really are crazy, you know that? You were going to sit through all of this just so I would stay?"

"Tell me I'm wrong."

He isn't. It's the perfect reason to get up and leave. If we aren't going to fuck, I have my out and I need to use it.

But I don't.

"You're wrong," I say, surprising us both. "I'll give you twenty-four hours."

He raises an eyebrow at me, skeptically. "Is this you conceding?"

"I'm compromising," I correct. "You have twenty-four hours to change my mind."

His mouth stretches ridiculously wide, and I can't help but mirror his smile.

It's unprecedented how badly I want to please this man. To be the guy he sees, be the guy worth chasing.

"If that's the case"—he quickly picks up his drink off the table and finishes it—"we need to get to my place sooner rather than later."

"Oh, so you do want to fuck me?" I tease.

"I told you," he says, rising up off his chair, sliding his wallet out of his back pocket and throwing down a handful of bills. "I'm going to feed you first."

"A true romantic," I joke. "I could've paid, you know."

Ignoring me, he extends his arm out and I take his hand, choosing to leave every single reservation behind in this dingy diner.

We don't hold hands as we head to the exit, but the proximity of his body to mine leaves no doubt in my mind that our physical chemistry is not the thing in question.

We walk back to the front of the club and Jesse guides us to the line of cabs waiting to take the crowd of people home at the end of the night.

Lowering his head, he looks into an open window and either asks the cab driver if he can take us or tells him his address. When he waves his hands over to me, I know it was the latter.

"It's only a short drive," he tells me, opening the back door of the yellow sedan. Tucking myself in, I slide across the back seat and watch Jesse and his thick thighs and long legs climb in. "I usually like driving everywhere," he continues. "But I was supposed to get shitfaced with my best friend Zara for her birthday."

"You bailed on your best friend's birthday?" I ask, a little shocked. "I hate to tell you, but you're a shit best friend."

He laughs, loud and rich. "She would agree with you, but lucky for me, she puts up with me, and I'm almost certain she won't be too upset when I tell her why. She's always on my case, telling me I need to meet someone."

"You don't look like someone who needs assistance in that department," I compliment.

"I'm not," he answers confidently. "But I'm picky."

"Do you live by yourself?" I ask him, moving the conversation far away from me.

"Yes," he answers. "It's not too big, but it's close to work and Zara and my daughter."

I turn my head to look at him, the shock on my face clear. "You have a daughter?"

"I do," he says cautiously. His eyes search my face before adding, "Is that a problem?"

"No." I shake my head vehemently. And it isn't. It isn't like we're playing house and she's going to call me Dad. "How old is she?"

"She's ten."

My brows furrow as I try and fail at math. "How old are you?"

"I'm twenty-six," he offers. He must see the concentration on my face when he adds, "Yes, I had her in my freshman year of high school."

"Holy shit," I breathe out. "I couldn't imagine raising a baby in high school."

"It was definitely an experience," he admits.

"She's not home now, is she?"

"My daughter? No." He chuckles. "She's staying at my parents' place tonight."

"Not with her mom?" I ask.

"You mean Zara?"

"Zara, your best friend?"

"Yeah," he clarifies, but not before the cab pulls into a driveway. I take note of the suburban surroundings and cozy-looking brick house.

Not wanting Jesse to pay again, I lift my hips up off the seat and drag my wallet out of my back pocket. I quickly extend my arm to the driver, handing him cash.

"Thanks, man." I tap the seat and then turn my body to face the door. Opening it, I slide myself out as Jesse steps out of the other side.

"I could've paid, you know," he says, repeating the exact words I said to him at the diner.

I ignore him. "So, how long have you lived here?"

We make our way up his driveway and I follow him up the two steps that lead to his adorable patio. There's a cute little outdoor loveseat and a vintage, Tiffany-blue, child-sized bike with black streamers on both handlebars and a little basket up front.

"A few years."

"Cute bike," I say as he pulls open the screen door.

"She hates it." He unlocks the main door. "But I'm still trying to convince her to keep it."

"She doesn't like bike riding?"

"She doesn't like riding *that* bike," he corrects. "Apparently it's too girly."

My mouth tips up in a half smile, imagining Jesse trying to reason with his daughter.

Jesse turns some lights on as I follow him inside, and my eyes can't help but dart all over his house. It's a complete contradiction to what I would expect from a twenty-six-year-old. It's homey and lived in. Every wall is covered with framed photos and artwork. But not just any artwork. He has, what I assume to be, every single thing his daughter had ever even attempted, all over the place.

There are finger paintings and colored handprints from every age. There are drawings of people and almost every animal known to man. They range from scribble to stick figures to full-bodied figures with labels. It's like watching his daughter grow up without ever meeting her.

I shift my gaze to Jesse to find him holding a pile of folded clothes, trying to tidy up.

"What are you doing?" I ask.

"Nothing," he says quickly. "Just wasn't expecting company."

I walk over to him and take the stack out of his hands and place it back down on the coffee table.

"Your house is lived in." I place my hands on his shoulders. "I like it."

And I do.

I like the way I know his family is his priority just by standing here. His love and adoration for his daughter is everywhere and it tugs at something buried deep within my chest.

Something I desperately need to stop from attempting to rise to the surface.

He reaches for me, his hands on my hips, his expression soft but serious. "Thank you for coming back here with me," he says.

I smile. "You didn't really give me much of a choice."

"I didn't, did I?" His eyes drop to my mouth and then back up again, nothing but want staring at me now.

Standing here like this is the closest we've been, outside the club, and it's already too much. The mood is changing, and the nerve endings in my body are dancing in anticipation.

Do I want him to kiss me?

My bravado is slipping, because here, in his house, I don't just want kissing. I want to get to know the man he is inside these four walls.

"Do you mind if I change?" he asks.

"Not at all."

He gives my hip a little squeeze. "I can find something for you too, if you want?"

I look down at my clothes, already imagining what it would feel like to wear something less constricting, but I don't really want to part with the only armor I have left against him.

"No, that's okay. I don't want to give you the wrong idea," I quip.

He chuckles, and I smile.

"I'll be back in five. Make yourself at home."

He didn't need to tell me twice. I watch him retreat around a corner and then continue my perusal of all the little clues the house has to offer.

If you had told me this family man and the man at the club were one and the same, I would've laughed in your face. But now his need to slow us down and dote on me the way he's been insisting, makes total sense.

It's obvious he's a caretaker and provider by nature. These four walls are proof of that.

My feet take me to the kitchen and right in front of his fridge. There are more kid paintings and a dry-erase whiteboard that looks like a worn down to-do list.

"If you can't tell, I can't chuck out a single thing she's created."

My body startles at the sound of his voice and I turn to

face him. "Damn," I breathe out, mesmerized by the sight of him. "You really look good in anything, don't you?"

Ignoring the compliment, he grabs me by the waist and guides me to a corner of the kitchen. "Let me make us something to eat. You can ogle me while I do it."

The man didn't have to twist my arm to get me to comply.

"Eggs, bacon, and pancakes okay?"

"Perfect," I reply.

Jesse glides his way around his kitchen, opening the fridge, grabbing ingredients from his pantry, and setting up three pans on his stove. I stand there salivating over him, just as he ordered, because the way his shirt hugs his muscles and his sweatpants hang on his hips have me wanting to get on my knees for him right in the middle of the kitchen.

"How do you want your eggs?" he asks.

I drag my eyes up his body and meet his gaze. "What?"

"Eggs," he repeats. "How do you like them cooked?"

"Oh. Um, scrambled will do."

He turns to face the stove and my eyes dart back down to his ass. I could easily sink my teeth into it.

"Have you gotten a good enough look?" he asks, without even looking at me.

"Honestly," I say, "I'm a little intimidated about how good you're going to look naked."

I watch him plate the eggs and the bacon and then face me. He walks to the set of drawers beside me, grabs cutlery, and casually hands me the food, like we do this every day.

"The pancakes are coming," he says.

I take the plate in one hand and then grab his forearm with the other. He looks down and waits for me, but I don't know what it is I want to say. Nobody has ever cooked me a meal, not with the intention to just feed me and me only.

"Thank you," I say, my voice low and reserved.

Brown eyes meet mine and I'm certain he can see right through me. How empty I am and how much more this means to me than he'll ever know. He raises his arm and I lose my hold on him. His large hand cups my face, his thumb skimming my bottom lip. Leaning in slowly, he presses his mouth to my cheek and then whispers, "You're welcome."

He walks back across the kitchen and starts making pancake batter with absolutely no precise measurements, more than likely a breakfast he's made for his daughter a million times before.

"Do you have any flaws?" I blurt out. "Because at this point, I'm certain you don't have any."

He turns around, beating the pancake mix, not the least bit put off by my question. "Are you going to eat?"

I lift a piece of bacon to my mouth and take a bite, still waiting for an answer.

"I'm stubborn," he answers before giving his attention back to the pancakes. "Detrimentally so."

I could see that. I'm in his house, eating bacon and eggs at midnight—I don't think taking no for an answer was even an option for him.

"What else?"

"Hold up." He turns on two burners and begins to pour the batter into two separate pans. "I want to know if you have any flaws."

I shake my head, even though he can't see me. "We do not need to go down that rabbit hole."

There's a lull in the conversation as I watch Jesse focus on pouring and flipping the pancakes, hoping we don't return to his inquisition. He places the last pancake on the stack and brings the full plate to my side of the kitchen. He puts it on the counter, and stands in front of me.

There's nothing but determination in his eyes as he curls his hand around the nape of my neck. I swallow and his thumb tracks the motion of my throat.

It's the simplest touch, but I feel it everywhere.

"Tell me," he demands.

His presence is both unnerving and intoxicating. I want to stay right here and flee all at the same time.

"I'm indecisive," I tell him. "I can't make a quick decision to save my life."

"So if I asked you if I could kiss you right now, what would your answer be?"

There's no doubt the answer is yes. I would kill to feel his lips on mine, but my indecision comes when I think about the consequences of the kiss.

My whole intention this evening has been a one-night stand, and something deep in my gut tells me if I let this man kiss me, I won't be able to walk away.

Am I ready for that?

Is he ready for someone like me?

His thumb continues skimming up and down my neck as he patiently waits for my answer.

"Hurry, our food's getting cold," he jokes.

And I appreciate the levity.

"I'm still unsure," I say honestly and then softly press my lips to his. "About all of this."

Jesse's hand gently squeezes my neck as he whispers against my mouth, "Luckily, I'm not."

CHAPTER FIVE

NOW

"JESSE." My boss's voice drags my head out from under the hood of a car I'm working on. "Zara called to tell you she picked Raine up from school early."

"What?" Straightening my back, I roll out my shoulders and tilt my head from side to side, hoping to rid myself of the stiffness. "Why didn't she just call my cell?" I ask, patting what I know now are my empty pockets.

"You probably left it in the break room, again," Deacon informs me. "I don't know why you bother having one when you never remember where you last left it. What if—"

"You're not my mother," I say, cutting him off. "I don't need that lecture today."

He shrugs. "Whatever. I told her you'd call her back."

Picking up a nearby rag, I wipe my hands down, despite them being permanently stained with oil and grease, and head out of the garage to retrieve my phone.

Walking into the break room, my palms start to feel clammy and my pulse quickens. It's an irrational response, one that I refuse to tell anyone about, but one I can't seem

61

to control as I acknowledge the whereabouts of my phone and pick it up off the counter.

Notifications fill up my screen, and despite *knowing* that they're from Zara and Raine, I can't seem to get my breathing under control.

It's been a whole year, and every time someone calls or texts me, it immobilizes me. Both physically and mentally, I'm back at my house in my kitchen answering the worst phone call of my life.

Now I want nothing to do with the damn thing.

Hence the "accidental" subconscious slip.

"Are they okay?"

Looking over my shoulder, I find Deacon in the doorway. "Are you stalking me?"

"I'm just checking you found your phone and spoke to Zara."

This man is a mother hen, and I'm certain he has no idea that's how he comes across. I don't mind it... when it isn't directed at me, but lately we don't go a whole day at work without him doing a—what he thinks is a subtle—mental health check in.

It's thoughtful, but I don't need them.

"I'm about to call her," I lie. "But I can't do that if you're talking to me."

He rolls his eyes at me. "If you're home alone tonight, you can come to dinner at our place."

"And be the third wheel to you and your husband?" I scoff. "No, thanks."

"Christy's out of town. I can get Wade to come."

I guess having Wade there without his wife, Christy, makes me less of an extra. I consider it for a second, because going home to an empty house, night after night, is taking a toll on me.

Somedays I do a really good job of hiding it.

Today clearly isn't one of them.

"Come on," Deacon coaxes. "Check in with Zara and get back to me."

I've been working at Duquette's for about two and a half years, after Deacon and Wade had turned their one-stop shop into a state-wide franchise. Hired to run their original workshop, while they continued to focus on their expansion, they both placed a lot of trust and faith in my abilities.

This, in turn, allowed us to become close, and these men are more than just the two people I work for. In the last twelve months, they stood by my side in more ways than I would have ever expected them to.

Along with their invitations to dinner, or Christy sending food with Wade to give to me, they gave me all the time I needed to process the things going on at home. I later learned that a few years back, after a back-and-forth battle with cancer, Deacon's younger brother had died.

Death doesn't discriminate, and grief is the roller coaster ride that everybody wants to get off.

It also unites strangers like nothing else.

There is some kind of solidarity to be found in the whole experience, in how a complete stranger can understand one of the most intimate heartaches of your life, without you even having to say a thing.

I couldn't imagine what it was like to lose a brother any more than he could imagine what it was like to lose a child, but a loss of someone you love, is a loss all the same.

I wave the phone in the air. "Let me get to this and then I'll get back out there and let you know."

He nods and retreats, leaving me to call Zara. But I don't. Instead, I skim through her texts noting, thankfully,

Raine needed to be picked up from school early to tighten her braces. An appointment they both forgot about.

I can't say it was always easy. When you have a child so young, you're often raising them and finding yourself along the way, and that was a reality for Zara and me.

And we navigated that well, until now.

For Raine's sake we're all trying to co-exist while simultaneously trying to give each other space. But it isn't working. I miss Zara.

I miss the ease of our relationship.

I miss the before while also being unable to regret the after.

And missing Leo makes it all so much worse.

We were a shell of the happy, positive, and supportive family we used to be.

Is it unconventional? Yes.

Did it work for us? Also, yes.

Which makes the collapse of it all an even harder pill to swallow.

Looking down at my phone, I pull up my messages app and let my fingers hover above the screen, deciding if I should send Leo a text. I know it'll go unanswered, but the die-hard romantic in me refuses to give up on him.

I'm still here, thinking of him every second of every day, and despite his constant silence and rejection, I need him to know that that won't ever change.

RELUCTANTLY, I DRAG MYSELF OUT OF THE WARM POOL AND welcome the cool air against my skin. While unwinding in the water has always been something I've done, these last few months, this pool has become my second home.

My mother used to tell anybody who listened that I was born to be in the water. When I was a baby you couldn't get me out of the bath, and when I learned how to swim you couldn't get me out of the pool.

I don't swim to compete.

I don't swim to stay fit.

I swim because when I'm in the water, everything else goes away. In the water I feel like I'm the best version of myself.

My slate is clean.

Whether it be the noise in my head, or the tension rolling through my body, the water brings peace and clarity that I am always grateful for.

Now, I was a thirty-three-year-old man whose short life had a long list of experiences. Over the years they have ebbed and flowed between high highs and some of the most crippling lows. And my relationship with the water has recently changed.

It could no longer keep me grounded.

It no longer held all the answers or soothed my body and mind while I sought them.

But it was my routine. And just like everything else in my life right now, I refuse to let it go.

I don't care if it makes me stupid or stubborn, but everything is changing so quickly, and I'm terrified of what will be left.

Left of my marriage

Left of my family.

Left of me.

It's another late afternoon of coming home to an empty house, and I don't know how much longer I can do it. It doesn't matter that he sleeps here every night; the absence between us is so profound I feel it every hour of every day.

A house without him hurts more than the thought of fighting with him.

At least if we're fighting, he'd be here.

No matter how angry he is, or how much his words hurt, I want him here. I don't believe in distance, I don't believe in taking a break. And he knows that.

AWKWARDLY, WITH A SIX-PACK OF BEER IN HAND, I KNOCK ON Deacon's apartment door, feeling a little out of place, but not enough to have declined the invitation.

"Hey, man." I turn to find Wade stepping out of the elevator just as Deacon opens the door.

"Oh, it's a real Duquette's reunion out here." He widens the door and gives us enough room to walk through. "How are you, fellas? Long time no see."

I raise the beer. "Want me to put it in the fridge?"

He tips his head in the direction of the kitchen. "Yeah, Julian is in there finishing up dinner."

Leaving him and Wade to talk shit in the doorway, I find Julian cutting up vegetables for a salad.

"Julian, hey," I greet.

He looks up from the chopping board. "Jesse. It's so good to see you." He eyes the six-pack. "Just pop it in the fridge. Bottom shelf should have room."

I follow his instructions, closing the fridge just as Wade and Deacon join us. They're still talking about work stuff, so I move closer to Julian and see if he needs a hand.

"No, I'm about done," he answers. "We didn't put much effort in tonight. I just made some spaghetti and meatballs with garlic bread and a salad for Deacon because he's on a no-carb diet."

It takes a few too many seconds before Julian's words register. "What? Since when?"

"A few weeks," he answers.

"You're not on a no-carb diet," I say loud enough to interrupt Deacon and Wade's conversation.

"Yes, I am."

Wade interjects, "No, you're not. I've seen you buy one of those gourmet sandwiches from the cafe across the street almost every day this week."

Deacon glances at Julian, who just laughs. "Why are you looking guiltily at me? I didn't tell you to go on a diet, you put yourself on one."

"It's not a diet," he clarifies. "It's a lifestyle change."

"It's not anything if you're still eating carbs," Wade adds.

"I'm just trying to be healthier and more fit for when the..." His voice trails off as he looks at me. And when Wade and Julian look at me with worry too, I know exactly what he was going to say.

"When the baby comes," I finish.

Sadness fills the room, and I hate that my presence and my past put it there.

People, especially Deacon and Julian, deserve to enjoy the highlights of life's journey. We all know of the fragility of life. One way or another, we've all had it slip through our hands, and being happy doesn't ever detract from that.

We are complex creatures, and grief and happiness can co-exist. I can hurt and long for and miss my baby, and that won't ever mean that I can't be elated for theirs.

"Did you find a surrogate?" I ask, knowing that was the route they were wanting to start their family with.

"Jesse, man," Deacon starts, and I put up a hand.

"Don't," I tell him. "I want you to be able to talk about it in front of me. It's not like I don't pick up bits of it here and there when I see you at work."

What I don't say is I crave the normalcy. Yes, life has moved on, but it feels like it has moved on around me and not with me.

I bounce my gaze between the three men. "You have all been there for me this last year. In ways that go above and beyond. At the very least I can handle hearing about your plans."

They don't seem convinced, but Julian at least nods in understanding and then hands Deacon a set of plates. "Help me set the table." He looks back at me. "We've got plenty of time to catch up."

Despite a rocky start, Julian and Deacon offer limited details about their surrogacy plans but enough that I don't feel like they're purposefully keeping their happiness away from me.

"And how are Raine and Zara?" Deacon asks. "Was everything okay after Zara called the garage today?"

"Oh, yeah," I reply. "They just forgot about an orthodontist appointment Raine had. She ended up sleeping at Zara's house instead of coming to mine after school like usual."

"Man, I know it's not really the same, but I grew up with divorced parents, and the way you and Zara make that work has me wishing you were my parents," Wade says.

I laugh because it isn't the first time we've been praised for our co-parenting. "I suppose it helps that romantic feelings have never been involved," I tell them. "And Zara and I were lucky enough to come from wholesome supportive families. They were firm about their expectations if we kept the baby, but they were equally supportive. We wanted to replicate that, and we were able to set the standard for our parenting very early. By the time we introduced anyone to Raine, they kind of had to fit in the fold or it wouldn't work."

"That feels like a tall order for any potential partners," Wade says. "I bet Leo felt like he was on the chopping block when he was about to meet Raine."

My mouth tilts up in a smile thinking about Leo and how adamant he was that I should not introduce him to Raine. "I think he was more scared he would get attached to Raine."

"I don't even have to ask if he got attached," Julian says. "I've seen them together."

My chest constricts at his words and my nose stings unexpectedly. I miss seeing them together. I miss the ease in which our family functioned, and even though I want to believe we will be able to pull ourselves out of this pit of despair, I'm sick of waiting for it to happen.

Every day feels like we're sinking further, and I'm certain at some point we're just going to be buried in it and getting ourselves out will no longer be an option.

Before I get the chance to wallow, my phone rings, the trill sound turning my body into stone.

My eyes find Deacon's and he's staring at me knowingly. I concentrate on my breathing as I slide the cell out of my pocket, but when I see Gio's name on the screen, my whole body wars with itself, unable to answer.

Deacon reaches over the table and pulls the phone out of my hand, answering it. These calls always have to do with Leo, and I don't know if I can handle one more pick up from our local bar.

I try to focus on his facial features, hoping to decipher the urgency of the call, and when Deacon's face falls, my arms and hands move on autopilot and snatch the cell out of his grasp.

"Gio," I say into the phone. "Where's Leo?"

"We're at the police station."

My brain scrambles, trying to land on any one reason they would be at the police station and I come up empty. "What do you mean you're at the police station?"

"He got arrested for drunk driving."

Gio's voice is as hollow as I feel.

When the fuck will this shit end?

"Gio," I breathe out, my whole heart in that one breath.

"I know, Jesse. I know."

When I can't find the words to continue the conversation, he adds, "I'll text you the address."

We both hang up, and I give myself a few extra seconds before I look up at the concerned men.

Swallowing hard, I clear my throat trying to rid myself of the golf-ball-sized lump that's just sitting there. "I've got to go."

I scoot my chair backward and rise. "Thank you for dinner."

Three sets of eyes just stare at me, and I have to turn away to avoid their pitying looks. I'm so fucking over it.

Unable to stand there any longer, I side step the chair, tuck it in, and turn to walk to the front of the apartment.

As I'm about to open the door, I remember one last thing. I glance over my shoulder to find Deacon hot on my heels. Just as I open my mouth to ask, he nods. "Come back to work when you can."

These people are too good to me.

"Thank you," I say softly.

By the time I'm in the car, I've put the address Gio sent through into my GPS and am speeding to get there. It's counterproductive and completely unhelpful, but I need to see him in the flesh.

When I arrive, Gio is waiting for me, leaning against his car, sucking on a cigarette for dear life.

"I thought you quit," I say to him.

"He makes me want to do drugs," he says matter-of-factly. "This is better than that."

Snatching the stick off him, I take a drag and try to wrap my head around the fact that I am standing outside a police station, when it dawns on me. The saddest chuckle leaves my mouth. "I'm guessing you were his one phone call?"

CHAPTER SIX

leo

THEN

"I CAN'T BELIEVE you're cleaning up," Jesse says.

We've moved past the first kiss and, much to his dismay, I'm now washing dishes in his sink.

"You just made a complete stranger a midnight breakfast, it's the least I can do." I place the last plate on the stainless steel rack and switch off the water. My eyes search the counters and, as if he can read my mind, Jesse offers me a dish towel.

"Thank you," I say with a smile, taking it out of his hand.

"Can I at least get you something comfortable to wear?"

"I already told you," I say. "If you want to get me into your bed, all you have to do is ask."

"Oh, I'm going to get you into my bed alright."

Catching me completely off guard, Jesse bends, wraps his arms around my waist, and throws me over his shoulder.

"What are you doing?" I shout while laughing. "Put me down."

He passes the living room, and I try to look over my

shoulder to see where he's taking us. I'm surprised when we walk into what I assume to be his bedroom.

He puts me down in the middle of the room and I take in the view.

It's simple.

A king-sized bed with blue monochromatic bedding sits in between two walnut bedside tables adorned with a simple wrought iron lamp on either one.

There is a matching cube shelving unit across from the bed and a flat screen TV mounted on the wall above it.

"It's like a man cave and a bedroom combined," I observe.

"In case you couldn't tell," he says, pointing to the door. "Out there is clearly my daughter's house and she allows me to share her space. Here"—he gestures around the room and walks toward a built-in wardrobe—"is the only thing that's really mine."

He pulls open the door, slides out the second drawer, grabs some clothes, and throws them on his bed.

"Wear them," he orders.

Realizing there really is no point in arguing with this man, I begin to unbutton my shirt and move closer to the bed. "You know your clothes are going to hang loose on me."

"You know you can wait till I leave the room to change," he replies.

Glancing up, I catch him leaning against the door, hand curled behind him, holding the doorknob, but his body faces me, like he has no intention of actually leaving the room.

"And where's the fun in that?" I tease, my fingers now moving down my shirt, my eyes on his, watching the way I'm tempting his resolve. "You said no sex tonight," I remind him. "I didn't say I wouldn't try to change your mind."

"Fuck," he mutters. "You're enjoying this, aren't you?

Smirking, I reach for the belt buckle on my pants, and Jesse pushes himself off the door, strides toward me, and puts his hand over mine. We both look down and my voice comes out in a hoarse whisper. "Are you stopping me? Or is this you wanting to undress me yourself?"

Lifting my head, I see the indecision written all over his face, the bob of his Adam's apple, and his inability to answer me. I watch his heated gaze travel down my half-exposed chest, and my dick thickens inside my pants, enjoying his fall from grace entirely too much.

Despite his hand covering mine, I slowly but skilfully unbuckle my belt. I give him enough time to intervene, but when his hand loses its grip, I undo the button and drag the zipper down, exposing my covered erection.

We stare at one another now and I raise an eyebrow, challenging him.

"Touch me," I whisper.

He shakes his head, but he grips the waistband of my pants in one hand, tugging me to him, and slips the other between my chinos and briefs, the heel of his palm grazing down the length of me.

Biting my bottom lip, I take in a shuddering breath and let my head fall back as he continues the motion. When I feel his lips against the hollow of my throat, I groan.

"Pants off," he murmurs before sucking at my skin. He moves his mouth up my neck and behind my ear as we work my chinos and underwear down my legs.

When I step out of them, he pushes me down onto the mattress, my open shirt now the only thing I'm wearing and my body propped up my forearms. My naked legs hang over the edge of the mattress and I wait for the shame or embarrassment to come, but it doesn't.

I'll be and do whatever he wants.

"You're going to regret this," he says, but before I get the chance to work out what he means, he drops to his knees and I feel the saliva pool in my mouth.

Still fully clothed, Jesse spreads my legs apart and settles his huge frame between them. He looks at me with the fire of a thousand suns in his gaze, and when both of his hands simply rest atop my thighs, I want nothing more than to burn for him.

He slides his hands higher up my legs till his hands are resting on either side of my groin.

"Touch yourself," he orders gruffly.

And without a single thought of my own, I sit up, spread my legs even wider, and eagerly obey him.

Motivated by his desire for me, my hand moves up and down, wanting nothing more than to be his puppet and for him to pull my strings. Jesse's gaze flicks between my cock and my face, and I don't know what I want him to look at more.

I keep working myself over, and pre-cum begins to pool at the tip of my cock. At the sight of it, Jesse's tongue glides over his bottom lip, and I don't even think twice as I stop stroking myself and swipe two fingers over my wet crown and hold them as an offering in front of his mouth.

I don't say a word.

I don't give him orders.

I just wait.

And when he grabs my wrist and covers my fingers with his mouth, I feel it all the way down to my toes. His tongue swirls around my two digits, the undiluted lust in his eyes undoubtedly mirroring mine.

Still holding me, he drags my fingers out of his mouth and then guides my hand to the bed beside my hip. He does the same on the other side, and before I can argue, Jesse is holding me hostage, my hands held down by him on either side of my hips.

"What are you doing?" I ask, even though it's very obvious.

Ignoring me, he says, "Spread your legs as far as they go."

Of course, I do, and somehow he manages to bring himself closer.

Still restraining me, Jesse's mouth starts at one knee and moves his way up my thigh. The kisses are soft, almost ghost-like, but goose bumps dot my skin and anticipation has my body humming.

He does this over and over, alternating legs, going all the way to my groin, to work his way back down again.

My dick hurts, straining and desperate, the blood rushing down my body at an unbelievable pace. "Jesse. Please," I groan, trying and failing to move my hands.

"Please what?"

"Touch me," I pant. "Or let me touch you. Fuck."

He lets go of my hands, but before I can reach for him, he shakes his head. "Uh uh. Keep them beside you."

And because I'm done for, I fist the comforter with both hands and wait.

"Is this what you want?" he taunts, rolling my balls in his hand. "Or maybe it's this?"

Without warning, Jesse grips my cock and covers it with his mouth.

"Fuck," I moan letting my head fall back. "Fuck. Fuck. Fuck."

He pulls off with a pop. "Rule number one: don't move your hands. And rule number two: don't fucking come."

The man might be on his knees for me, sucking my cock, but right now it's me and my body made to serve him. Despite the default urge to rush to my orgasm, his demand that I deny myself release is somehow the bigger prize.

"God, you weren't lying were you," he says gruffly, one hand on my leaking cock, the other pinching my nipple. "Your body really is a sight."

I'm a live wire under both his touch and his compliments.

"I bet you're even prettier when you come."

My hips buck at his words and I want to show him just how fucking pretty I can be.

"Easy," he coos. "Patience."

His mouth is back on me, lips sliding up and down my shaft, his tongue rolling around the head. His big hand effortlessly rolls my balls, and the tips of two fingers dip lower and press against my taint.

It feels like heaven and hell and everything in between.

"Jesse," I call out. "I'm gonna come."

It wasn't like I'd never jerked off with another guy before. I enjoy foreplay just as much as the fucking, but whatever this is with Jesse, it will ruin me for every man who comes after him.

Sliding his mouth off my cock, he licks his lips before reaching for me. With a hand on the back of my neck, he slams his lips against mine.

This kiss is nothing like the one we shared in the kitchen. It's not the tentative greeting of two men willing to get to know each other. With the taste of myself on his tongue, this is undeniable greed and lust.

Reluctantly, Jesse pulls away from me and an embarrassing whimper slips out of my mouth.

I want to come, but I also don't want this to stop.

His gaze on me is hungry and feral as he surprises me and stands up. He pushes down his sweats and underwear, revealing his impressive cock, and straddles me.

My body collapses against the mattress on instinct as Jesse hovers over me, one hand on his cock, the other stopping him from falling on me.

He begins stroking himself, a torturous but seductive rhythm, every slide of his hand accentuating his impressive size. Watching him drives me insane. My own cock is painfully hard, my body so wound up I feel like a grenade ready to explode.

I am so turned on by how little he is actually doing to me and how much I'm affected by it all. Just when I think he's serious about the orgasm denial, he releases his hold on himself and wraps his hand around the both of us and begins to relentlessly fuck his fist.

My hips buck off the bed and I match him for every thrust. It's a sticky mess between us, filth of the very best kind.

A sheen of sweat covers my skin as heat coils at the base of my spine and my balls tighten. My back arches off the bed and I feel myself coming undone.

"That's it," he rasps, stroking us through our orgasms. "Show me how fucking pretty you are."

CLEAN AND SATED, I CLIMB INTO JESSE'S BED LIKE A LIMP NOODLE, finally dressed in the clothes he pulled out for me earlier, and make myself comfortable under the blankets. It's now early morning, and while I feel somewhat tired, my brain is racing a million miles a minute.

We showered together, but it was a relaxed, comfortable silence. Almost like a strange sense of shyness had settled between us as his hands washed my body and mine washed his.

Sex was just supposed to be sex. And from what I've gathered, Jesse and I view it very differently. I'd had a lot of it, and his encounters seemed to be few and far between. I'm not sure if it's the actual act that matters to him or who he does it with, but I'm certain neither of us has ever experienced chemistry as intense as what we shared earlier.

The bedroom door swings open, interrupting my thoughts, and Jesse walks in, his towel-dried hair pointing every which way, carrying two bottles of water, and a satisfied smile spread wide across his face.

I feel my own smile start to grow, so I grab a throw pillow and bury my face in it before he sees how big and goofy it is.

I hear him place the bottles down before the bed dips and the pillow is dragged away from me.

"This is how you looked in the club," he states.

I snatch the pillow back off him. "What are you talking about?"

"When you were attempting to do that thing you call dancing," he clarifies.

"You mean when I *was* dancing?"

Chuckling, he shakes his head. "Baby, that was not dancing."

I shrug off the endearment, because it sounds so good, and if I'm not careful, at the end of our twenty-four hours I'm going to be throwing myself at Jesse's feet, begging him to keep me.

"What are you talking about?" I climb out of the bed and grab my cell phone that sits on one of his nightstands. Shuffling through one of my playlists, I click on a pop song I'm certain was playing tonight. "This is how everybody dances," I tell him.

I wait for the chorus to kick in and I start throwing my arms around and shaking my hips just like I did in the club.

"Oh my god," he laughs. "Who the hell taught you how to dance?"

"It caught your eye, didn't it," I tease.

I continue to move, laughing with him, and Jesse lunges for me, grabbing me around the waist and carrying me to the middle of the bed. He lies on top of me, and I spread my legs so he can settle in between.

Propping himself up with his forearms, he just stares down at me.

"You have the most beautiful smile," he says matter-of-factly before dropping the softest kiss on my lips. "That's what caught my eye first."

I don't know why his revelation has a lump forming in my throat, but I am so floored by his honesty and willingness to just lay it all out there. There has been nothing but complete transparency from the beginning, and I didn't realize how refreshing it would be.

He isn't playing a game and he isn't scared of rejection. He isn't working his way through an endless number of one-night stands because the idea that someone could get to know him scares the complete shit out of him.

No. That's just me.

"What's got you thinking so hard?" he asks.

"You," I answer honestly.

"And?"

"What happens when the twenty-four hours are up?" I ask. "What happens when I walk out this door later today?"

For some reason, the second the questions leave my mouth I think of his best friend and his daughter and this house that's covered in a child's love letters to her father.

"I told you I needed twenty-four hours to convince you that this could be more," he states. "If I do that correctly, then you know it doesn't matter what happens when you walk out the door, because you know, whenever you want to, you'll be able to walk right back in."

I run my thumb across his bottom lip. "You know nothing about me."

"And only you can change that," he challenges.

"I don't have a family," I blurt out, purging my deepest darkest secret first. If I tell him the ugly things first, it'll give him a chance to leave without investing too much time into this. We would only be losing tonight.

My heart cinches at the thought, but I ignore it. My heart and I had lived through much worse.

"My parents are alcoholics," I reveal. "They're mean drunks who struggle to do anything else but hate me."

His face softens at my admission, silently comforting me enough to continue. "Their abuse wasn't physical, but it hurt all the same, and when I turned eighteen, I got myself the fuck out of there. I have never looked back and I don't have a single regret."

My voice is shaking now, but I can't seem to stop the words from tumbling out. "I am truly the happiest I've been in a long time," I confess. "But it doesn't mean that every now and then it still isn't a struggle."

If Jesse wasn't on top of me, this would be the moment that I bolt. That I drop the news and run. As if he can sense my unease, he just kisses me.

And every time it's like the first time.

A new way to kiss.

A new way for our mouths to talk.

A new way for all the unsaid words to come out.

My hands find the edge of his t-shirt and I slip them underneath, holding his hips to me, feeling his skin.

My hands travel from his sides and slide beneath the waistband of his sweats. He's bare underneath and my hands cup the perfect globes of his ass and press him to me, feeling his cock thicken against mine.

The kiss deepens as our arousal heightens, but Jesse and I don't rock against each other. We don't seek the friction or chase the high.

With his lips on mine, we just exist.

One man confessing his truth, the other one absolving him of the burden.

I know, in this moment, with this kiss, there will never be another man in my life like Jesse. Whether we extend our twenty-four hours or not, the damage is already done.

I am irreparably changed.

And I know he is too.

CHAPTER SEVEN

leo

NOW

"AND YOUR CAR has been taken to the impound," the attorney Gio called for me says. "You'll be able to pick it up after your hearing."

Sobered up and nodding, I sign my release papers and pick up my belongings. I slip my wallet and phone into my back pocket and fold the handful of papers that hash out the consequences of tonight's events.

My head is pounding. I need to drink a gallon of water, shower this disgusting place off me, and sleep for a good two days straight.

We exit the processing area and the attorney adds, "I was told your husband is waiting for you."

"Oh, no, he's not my..." But it is Jesse there waiting for me. Not Gio.

I want to be mad at Gio, but the look on Jesse's face pushes everything else to the side.

I thought I'd seen every one of his looks there was to give, but this one is new.

This is disappointment.

Disappointment in *me*.

Shame prickles at the back of my eyes and coils in the pit of my stomach. It's a familiar emotion, but one I haven't felt often since my teens.

I reach him and he can barely look at me, and that alone feels like he's shoved his hand inside my chest and ripped out a chunk of what's left of my heart and threw it on the floor. It's so hypocritical of me to be hurt when I'm the one doing the hurting. Constantly.

Wordlessly, he heads toward the exit and I just follow him, subtly looking around the parking lot for Gio and his car.

"Sorry," he says, as we reach the car, disdain dripping from the single word. "He went home. I know I'm not the man you called to help you out or pick you up, but I'm what you got."

"Jesse," I breathe out, the plea in my voice obvious to both of us. But he doesn't even glance up at me as he unlocks the car and climbs inside.

It's not like I don't deserve his hostility, but the role reversal is so unexpected. I'm stunned.

Opening the passenger door, I lower myself into the seat and try to think of something to say to him, but I have nothing.

The tension between us is so thick it's suffocating, but I know I owe him *something*.

"Jesse," I repeat.

"Don't," he grits out. "Don't say my name like that. I do not want to hear you say my name without the anger and the hostility you've been slinging at me for a fucking year. Not tonight."

I slouch into the car seat, the shame from earlier returning. He's right. So right, but I don't know what else to do. I don't even know how to apologize.

What would I even be apologizing for? Tonight? Every night?

"What were you even doing?" he bellows, slamming his hand on the steering wheel. "Drinking and driving? Since fucking when, Leo? Self medicating is one thing, but you could've killed someone. You could've killed yourself."

I don't miss the hitch in his voice as the last statement leaves his mouth, and like a knife, the guilt cuts through my chest, deep and lasting.

"Jesse, please," I cry.

Shaking his head, he turns on the car and concentrates on pulling out of the parking lot. He doesn't want to hear it tonight, but I vow to myself that for the first time in a long time we will talk about it.

Fifteen minutes later, Jesse asks, "What did Gio's attorney say?"

There was no doubt in my mind that Jesse had harassed every single police officer who came within a five-foot radius of him, asking what had happened, how they found me, if I was okay, and how long it would be till I came out and he could take me home.

But I knew none of their answers would appease him as much as hearing it all out of my own mouth.

"My car is at the impound," I tell him. "And I have my hearing in two days. I'll ask Gio to come with me," I say quickly. "You don't need to take a day off work."

"Fuck that," he grits out. "You're my fucking husband. You need something, you ask me."

When I don't answer or argue, he quickly glances at me and then back at the road. "Why can't you call me?" he asks, his voice now calmer. "Please, Leo, say something."

"I know I'm a lot right now," I admit. "I do have the decency and enough self-awareness to know that."

"You're mine," he says with such finality. "You're *my* worry, *my* heartache, *my* burden. Whatever *you* think you are, whatever season it is for us, you're fucking *mine*, Leo."

It's the most heartbreakingly romantic thing he's said to me yet.

"We'll go to the hearing together," I say, surprising us both.

He purses his lips together and nods. "Now tell me why you were driving under the influence."

My limbs feel heavy at the thought of answering his question. At the thought of trying to make it all make sense to him.

"I went to see Lola," I confess.

"You drink at her grave," he accuses.

"No, I don't fucking drink at her grave," I snap back, my hackles rising. "But I visit her. A lot."

"I know," he says quietly. "I've seen you there a few times."

"You have? You've never said anything."

He scoffs. "It didn't seem like something you wanted to talk about."

I feel the dig. I deserve it.

I notice we're pulling into our driveway, and like the coward I am, I steer the conversation elsewhere.

"Is Raine asleep?"

"She's not here tonight," he says.

"But it's Wednesday."

"I know what day it is." He turns off the ignition and opens his door. "She had an orthodontist appointment and decided to stay with Zara tonight instead."

As much as I hate being home, I hate the thought of Jesse being alone in that house even more. Knowing Raine is there three out of the seven nights, sometimes maybe more, thins out my guilt just a little.

I climb out of the car and purposefully walk into the house slower than Jesse. This is the part of every night I hate the most. The reason I run to sit with Lola, almost every day. The reason I prefer to sit in a bar with strangers at night.

By the time I walk inside, I notice the house is still cloaked in darkness. I turn on the living room light just in time to see our bedroom door close; the wall both literally and figuratively being resurrected once again between us.

Unsure of what I'm going to say or even if I would say anything at all, I kick off my shoes and walk to our bedroom and place my hand in the middle of the door.

I imagine this is what Jesse looks like every morning, standing outside the guest room, warring with himself, wondering if that will be the day I would answer when he knocks.

But I don't knock. I don't know if it's the remaining alcohol in my system or maybe there is a full moon out, turning everything on its axis. But I barge into our bedroom, catching Jesse as he's undressing, with his shirt off and jeans undone, sitting low on his hips.

Words catch in my throat as I just stare at him. It's been so long since I've been this close to him, and the complete disarray my body is feeling is proof of that.

My hands want to reach for him. I want to feel his skin against mine as I run my fingers over the contours and grooves of his chest.

I want his arms around me to comfort and hold me.

I want to be loved and cherished in a way only he knows how to do.

God, I miss him, and when I finally manage to tear my

eyes away from his body, I see the need and turmoil in his eyes mirror my own.

"Is everything okay?" he manages to ask, his voice hoarse and tired.

"I..." My mouth opens and closes, my words stuck.

Swallowing hard, I try again.

"I wasn't trying to kill myself," I say softly.

I see the way my words hit him unexpectedly, the shift in his expression, the straightening of his spine. He walks toward me, and I feel myself retreating at his imposing proximity; a complete contradiction to the closeness I wanted to feel only seconds ago.

My heart beats in a rapid, almost painful, succession. Faster and faster the closer he gets.

His body is only inches away from mine as he reaches behind me and swings the door closed. He moves closer, forcing me to step backward until I hit the wall and his arms are boxing me in.

"Say it again," he demands.

It takes every ounce of strength I have to hold his gaze and repeat it. "I wasn't trying to kill myself." My voice comes out strained, my eyes welling up, my bottom lip trembling. "It's been hard," I croak. "And I'm not coping," I admit. "But tonight, that wasn't what I was doing. I don't think like that anymore."

"But you did?" he whispers. I half-shrug, allowing a tear to fall. "And you don't now?"

The word doesn't even have a chance to leave my mouth. Jesse slams his lips to mine, capturing my broken whimper.

I know better than to kiss him back. We are the messiest and ugliest versions of ourselves, and nothing good will come of it. But there is no end in sight. Our hearts continue to break, and I need my husband.

"Come here," he suggests.

I start to pull back, but he just grabs my hand and leads the way. I haven't slept in the bed or next to Jesse since Lola died—I truly don't even know if I can.

He surprises me when he detours to our en suite bathroom.

Still half dressed, Jesse leans into the shower and turns it on. The water runs as he turns to face me.

"Let's get you cleaned up first."

Jesse slowly and methodically takes all my clothes off. My shirt and jacket come off first. He gets down on one knee and removes the socks from my feet.

My body prickles in awareness at his proximity to the lower part of me, and when he begins to undo the buttons on my pants, my half-hard bulge is difficult to hide.

Steam fills the bathroom as Jesse drags my pants down my legs and helps me step out of them.

I'm completely naked now.

Extending his arm, he checks the water temperature and then leads me under the spray.

The next thing he does is so quintessentially Jesse, it shouldn't surprise me.

Still with his jeans on, he follows me into the shower and proceeds to wash me. He starts off with my hair, washing and rinsing the unruly mess. His pants are saturated now, but he just continues to soap up my body from head to toe.

He's on his knees now, and my length is rock solid, my body only having one single response when it comes to Jesse's touch.

With water rivulets running down his face, he looks up

at me, his hair wet, his eyelashes glistening, and a longing in his gaze that makes my dick jolt.

When his hand stalls at my groin, I grab his wrist and position it on my cock.

If he's surprised, he doesn't show it, instead wrapping his soap-covered hand around me and immediately gliding it up and down.

My head falls back into the spray and a small groan leaves my mouth as my climax threatens to approach all too quickly. It's been too long and my body is starved for his touch more than I need a release.

His hands alternate between caressing and squeezing, and I keep my eyes closed and revel in the moment.

A hand grips my hip and spins me around, and I move for him or with him, at this point, I don't care. Placing my palms on the tiled wall, I hang my head low, the water running through my hair and down my face.

I stifle a whimper when he pulls my cheeks apart and runs a digit along my taint.

Dancing up and down my crease, his finger teases my hole. When he slips it inside, I hold my breath and press my forehead to the cool tiles.

My cock is painfully hard, but the sadistic part of my personality refuses to touch myself. I welcome the torture just as much as I welcome his touch.

The silence between us is loud, and the recklessness of what we're doing is even louder.

This isn't smart; it isn't even stupid—it's dangerous.

We're playing with fire, but as Jesse stretches me wider with a second finger, I ask myself, *who cares?*

He continues to push his fingers inside me, deeper and harder, pegging my prostate with every thrust, just the way he knows I like.

I feel the familiar heat running up and down my spine, and despite not wanting to lose his touch, I grip my cock and fuck my fist. Furiously.

I'm unraveling, all the pent-up emotions rising to the surface as my body threatens to explode. Jesse matches my pace, pushing in three fingers, the pain-induced pleasure between us now turning angry and desperate.

This is a far cry from the way it started, but it's the only way it would end.

Jesse suddenly slides his fingers out of me, spreading my cheeks farther apart, and eases the sting caused by his fingers with an unexpected swipe of his tongue.

I can't handle any more.

I have no choice but for it to be over.

Every single one of my muscles tightens as Jesse continues with the punishing assault of his tongue. My body trembles at the arrival of my impending release and I bite the inside of my cheek to stop a loud moan from leaving my mouth.

Ropes of cum paint my hand as the wall in front of me becomes my own personal support person. I press my cheek to the tile, hoping for relief while I try to catch my breath.

I am spent.

Physically and mentally, I have reached a threshold I didn't even know I had.

I can still feel Jesse's presence in the shower with me, but I can't will myself to turn around and look at him. I am too raw to deal with the aftermath of whatever this is.

But even then I don't know if I want him to stay or go.

"Here," I hear him say. He comes up behind me, surprising me when he kisses my shoulder gently and hands me a soaped up loofah. "I'll get you a towel."

Because I have no self-control, I glance over my shoulder and watch him exit the shower. I stare at the back of him as he drags his saturated jeans past his perfectly toned ass, showing off his beautifully muscled body, if just for a second.

When he wraps a towel around his waist, I remember I'm supposed to be cleaning cum off myself, and I give my body a quick once-over and then turn off the water.

When I turn back around, Jesse has left the bathroom and a clean towel and a stack of clothes are ready for me on the nearby rack. I dry myself and try to anticipate what it'll be like when I walk back into our room.

Between my confession and the shower, I don't know where we stand.

So much was said, but even then it didn't even scrape the surface.

Quickly, I dry my body and get dressed in the lounge pants and t-shirt Jesse picked for me. When I find the courage to walk back into the room, I'm surprised to see he's still in a towel as he places a glass of water and a bottle of Tylenol on the nightstand.

"What're those for?" I ask.

"I didn't know if you needed some water after tonight, and I figured some Tylenol couldn't hurt."

"You didn't have to. I could've—"

He cuts me off when he steps closer to me, and I can't help but reach for him, my hands landing on his waist. The unmissable sharp intake of his breath reminds me just how much damage the last year has done.

He cradles my face and his thumbs gently skate back and forth over my cheeks. "I'm so glad you're here," he whispers. "That you decided to stay."

I know he doesn't mean here in this room, but rather

here and living, in general. It's a huge thing to admit, but I'd be lying if I said I didn't already feel pounds lighter.

"I'm going to grab some clothes and have a shower in the hall bathroom," he informs me.

My eyes dart between the bedroom door and our own bathroom door, quizzically. "You can have one here," I suggest.

"I know," he answers simply. "But I'm going to call it a night and sleep in the guest room."

Now I couldn't hide my confusion if I tried. "Jesse, this is your bed."

"It's *our* bed," he corrects. "And I want you to sleep in it."

"Without you?"

A humorless laugh leaves his mouth. "The irony, right?"

"You could stay."

"I know." He drops a kiss on the corner of my mouth. "But tomorrow you'll be a different man, and it's going to hurt enough without adding a whole night in bed with you."

CHAPTER EIGHT

jesse

NOW

"THEY CAN'T BE SERIOUS," Leo says into his cell as we enter the house. He tugs at his tie and alternates the phone between each shoulder and ear as he rolls up the sleeves of his button-down. Switch out his dress pants and shoes and he looks almost the same as he had the night I met him.

His curls were now wild; an untamed mess. I don't think he's cut it since Lola died. The lines on his face are a little older and deeper, but he is still the most beautiful man in any room.

"Outpatient rehab," he tells Gio. "It's some kind of joke, that's what it is. And to top it off, they're suspending my license for six fucking months."

Upon hearing the last part, I tip my chin up at him to get his attention. "Tell Gio whenever he's got time, he and I can go pick up your car from the impound."

"Did you hear that?" he asks Gio. He gives me a quick nod, letting me know he's passed on the message, and then continues to explain the details of his hearing to his best friend.

If he were Raine, I would gently remind him that irresponsible actions have consequences, but he isn't, and with the state our marriage is in, I don't think I'm the person he wants to hear it from anyway.

We're in some new phase after the other night. A lot has happened and a lot has been said, and we are far from being fixed, but yesterday was the first morning he got out of bed before I left for work.

I didn't want to read into it, but I also allowed myself to revel in the small win.

Leo continues to talk to Gio, and I almost feel myself tune him out when he mutters,

"It's as if I'm some kind of fucking alcoholic. I fucking know what an alcoholic looks like."

I don't know what Gio says to him from the other end of the line, but when his gaze meets mine, I know it's too late to hide the thoughts that are written all over my face.

"Gio," he says, while staring at me. "I'll call you back."

Any small win I thought I had is about to be eliminated.

We're both standing in the living room now, staring at each other. There's a storm brewing, anger and hurt and a whole lot of betrayal.

"You think I'm an alcoholic?" he asks bluntly.

Scrubbing a hand over my face, I sit down on the nearest couch. Leaning forward, I rest my forearms on my thighs and look up at him. "What do you want me to say here?"

He looks perplexed. "Obviously the truth."

When I continue to stare at him, no words leaving my mouth, he asks me again, "Do you think I'm an alcoholic?"

"Tell me why you think you're not," I throw at him, turning the tables.

"I can't believe this," he seethes. "Driving drunk doesn't mean I'm an alcoholic."

Rising up off the couch, I leap forward, managing to grab his arm. "You know this is so much more than what happened the other night."

He shakes himself out of my hold. "I'm going for a walk," he announces.

"Will you stop by a bar on your way?" I antagonize. "Drink just enough to say you're not drunk," I taunt. "Just enough to definitely not have to deal with anything real, right?"

This conversation is a big deal—for him to hear and me to say.

I've been tiptoeing around the inevitable since he started drinking. I let him be because who am I to judge his grief, but I knew better and turned a blind eye anyway.

I'm worried about whether or not we can handle one more thing. How much more can we take before the brunt is too heavy for us to hold? But the floodgates are open now and I need to let the river flow.

"I'm going for a walk," he repeats, his face and eyes now completely devoid of any emotion. He's shut me out. Again.

Sighing, I drop back down to the couch. "I'll be here."

And we both know I don't just mean when he comes back from his walk.

I'm just about to get up and change out of the clothes I wore to the courthouse when the front door opens.

My heart stutters as I look up expecting to see Leo, but my eyes land on Zara and Raine instead, and the organ in my chest thrums out a mangled rhythm.

There isn't a day I'm alive that I don't want to see my

daughter. But right now I need Leo, more than I need air, to be the person standing in my doorway.

"Hey, Dad," Raine greets, completely oblivious.

"Hey, babe."

Zara follows behind her, but her eyes take notice of my clothes and then nervously dart around the house.

"He's not here," I inform her, knowing very well how strained it is when she and Leo are in the same room.

Rising, I walk over to Raine, who's made her way to the kitchen, and kiss her on the top of the head. "How are you?"

The mood in the house is somber.

It doesn't matter who's here or who isn't here anymore, these four walls have never felt more void of the love and warmth we all spent years cultivating as they do right now.

"I'm good," she answers. "Mom and I spent the afternoon at the Space Needle."

Chuckling, I stand behind her as she takes a seat on the kitchen stool. I wrap my arm around her neck and rest my chin on the top of her head. "Are you two attending school and work anymore?" I joke.

Raine is obsessed with people watching. She hasn't yet fallen in love with the beauty found in simple things, and because we live in the suburbs, she finds it extremely fascinating to ask us to spend all our free time downtown, ticking off the Lonely Planet's Top Things to do in Seattle.

I'm certain she's going to be a travel and lifestyle reporter.

"Why isn't Papa home?" she asks. Hearing her call him that sucker punches me in the stomach without even realizing it.

Right after we got married, he was reciting stories of his own childhood—the happier memories—to her, referring to his grandfather as Papa, and one day she decided that's what she wanted to call him too.

"What?" I say dumbly, trying to bide time.

"I heard you tell Mom he wasn't here," she explains. "Where is he?"

Well, isn't that the million-dollar question.

"He had to go out," I lie. "Uncle Gio needed his help on something."

Poor Uncle Gio. I'll have to thank him for being the one person's name I can drop without Raine asking me any further questions.

She's too intuitive, and at times like this, I try everything to shield her from the hard truths. But when she has complete freedom to spend as much or as little time at our house as she wants, there's only so much I can hide.

Still holding Raine, my eyes follow Zara as she finally takes a seat on one of the recliners, curling her legs up underneath her and hugging a throw pillow to her chest. Closing her eyes, she looks small and sad, and my worry, as usual, just transfers from her to Leo and back again.

We are all hurting, but sometimes it feels like I'm the only one keeping us all together. I'm the middle man, and today I'm in agony underneath the weight of everyone's pain.

I'm the fixer. The protector. And I love being that person for my family... But lately, it feels like I'm failing because I can't fix or protect anybody. Especially them.

"Are you getting enough rest?" I ask Zara.

"She isn't," Raine pipes in. "I found her crying in the bathroom the other night."

"Raine," Zara scolds. "I did that in the privacy of my own home, and I would appreciate it if you didn't tell your dad my business."

"So, now I'm only her father," I quip, annoyed that she doesn't want me to know she's struggling.

"That's what you are," she says.

"We've been best friends our whole lives, and if you're struggling or you need help, you can tell me."

Her gaze darts to Raine and then back to me, pleading to let this go.

And I do, for Raine's sake.

"Can you at least go and nap?" I ask.

"I can have a nap at home," she argues.

Raine ignores us and untangles herself from my arms. "I'm going to have a shower."

Zara waits for Raine to walk out of earshot and then says, "What's with your outfit? No work today?"

Looking down at my pressed shirt and pants, I figure there's no use trying to hide the truth. "Gio called me the other night," I start. "He was at the police station with Leo, who got arrested for drinking and driving. We had the hearing today."

Her eyes widen. "Why didn't you tell me it was this bad?"

Shrugging, I raise my hands in defeat. "You're crying in the bathroom, Z. I don't need to add to that."

Even without the crying, I've been doing my best to keep as much as I can from her. She already holds so much guilt for losing Lola, and I make a conscious effort not to add my marriage to her list of casualties.

"I thought we didn't have secrets," she says.

She's right. We don't.

Usually we have a solid foundation when it comes to both our friendship and our roles as co-parents. But recently things have been blurred and messy. I'm trying to respect the privacy, pain, and healing of both her and Leo.

But it isn't working. We're all hiding feelings to spare the others and telling ourselves that the sadness we've all been cloaked in for the last twelve months will eventually go away.

It was taking its sweet-ass time.

"I can handle hearing about anything," she argues. "I want to be here for you."

Shaking my head, I effectively shut down the conversation. We don't need to rehash how much we all love one another and who did what and wanted to for whom.

We're family. We both know how this works. And knowing she has my back if I need it is enough.

Meeting Zara at the recliner, I extend an arm out and pull her up. Silently, I lead her to Raine's room.

It's a typical teenager's room, her finger paintings and childhood memorabilia now replaced with posters of places she wants to see, music she listens to, and random poems.

Pulling back the blankets, I wait for her to crawl into the bed, then tuck her in. Just like I would with Raine.

"I don't want to cause any trouble for you and Leo if he comes back and I'm still asleep," she says.

I kiss her forehead. "Let that be my problem."

She sighs but closes her eyes anyway and moves around, finding a comfortable spot.

Content that I'm able to take care of Zara for a few hours, I retreat to the hallway and close the bedroom door. Raine exits the bathroom, dressed in sweats and an over-sized t-shirt, her hair cocooned in a towel on the top of her head. "Your mom is sleeping in your room, okay? Try and keep the noise down to a minimum. Better yet," I add. "Do you want to help me prepare for dinner tonight? Since you and your mom are here, I figured I could make one of your favorites."

Her nose scrunches up. Raine loves eating the food, but she most definitely hates cooking it.

"I might lie next to Mom and read," she says thoughtfully. "Make sure she's okay."

In any other circumstances it would be my daughter avoiding the kitchen, but this time, I know she's genuinely concerned, which leaves me with a familiar sense of pride over my daughter's emotional maturity.

Nodding, I squeeze her shoulder and leave her to it.

When I hear her bedroom door close, I make my way out to the yard and drag my cell out of my pocket. No new notifications.

As usual, it's silence from Leo.

Groaning in frustration, I throw my phone on the nearby pool lounger and unbutton my shirt, peeling it off me. I toe off my dress shoes and yank my socks off my feet before undoing my pants, dragging the zipper down and shoving them to the ground.

I grab a nearby pair of shorts I must've left out to dry, change into them, jog to the pool, and dive in.

My body skates just a little above the bottom for the length of the pool. I somersault under the water and push against the wall, wanting to stay down for as long as I possibly can.

My lungs begin to burn, and still I would rather this feeling than dealing with the unresolved tension in our house right now.

When I can't take it any longer, I break through the surface and gasp for air.

"Someone would think you're the one trying to kill yourself under there."

Leo's voice startles me, but I take a moment before turning around. Months of well rehearsed self-preservation force me not to show him just how relieved I am he's back so soon.

I sink underneath the water and turn, popping my head up to face him.

He's sitting on the edge of the pool, shoes and socks off, pants awkwardly rolled up. My breath hitches and my chest cinches at the sight. He used to do this when it was too cold to join me.

"Zara and Raine are here," I say, choosing to get any further discomfort out of the way.

"I know, I saw Zara's car in the driveway."

"They're both asleep. Raine mentioned Zara is having a rough time," I explain. "And I would rather she stay here than be home alone."

"Jesse Hunt, always the caretaker," he says sarcastically. I see him wince as soon as the words leave his mouth.

"It's Ricci-Hunt," I correct. "We're married, remember? And someone's got to take care of you."

"And you take care of me because we're married or because I'm an alcoholic?"

"Are you?" I ask, dismissing the way he tries to have a subtle dig. It's the second or third time he's avoided answering the hard question, and I refuse to be the one to tell him my version of events and have them be his truth.

If we have any hope of getting through this, I need him to have his own moments of truth and clarity.

They can't be mine.

Especially not when it comes to his drinking.

"Is she alright?" Leo asks, ignoring the question and making me angry for a different reason.

I dunk my head under the water, count to ten, then push my body to the other side of the pool.

When I come up for air, I'm directly in front of Leo. An arm's length away.

"I asked if Zara was okay," he reiterates.

"Since when do you care about Zara?"

He flinches, and I try to push away the guilt that my honesty carries.

It's been a year of us dancing around each other, me more than him. Too scared to rock the boat. Too scared to push him away any farther.

But things are changing. His DUI has become a catalyst for all the things we've left unsaid and the perfect example of all the ways this could blow up in our faces. The reality is the consequences of his one mistake are too big to be walking around on eggshells anymore.

"You know I've always cared about Zara," he answers, bringing me back to the present.

This time I bite my tongue. I don't sling my own hurt back at him and tell him he hasn't cared for a single person since the day Lola died.

Not Zara.

Not Raine.

And especially not me.

Instead, I say something that hurts us both even more. "Do you think you can get Gio to pick you up? I don't think you should be here when Zara wakes up."

CHAPTER NINE

leo

THEN

"ARE you sure it isn't too soon?" I ask.

"For you to marry me?" he responds. "Absolutely not."

Contradictory to the words that leave my mouth, I can't help the size of the smile that spreads across my face.

"Jesse," I scold. "It's been three months. It's undoubtedly too soon for you to even utter the word marriage, let alone be so sure."

Without even looking at me, he reaches over the console and places his hand on my thigh and squeezes. "When you know, you know. But to answer your question, no, it is not too soon for you to meet Zara. I've met Gio. What's the difference?"

"Well, for one, Gio and I don't have any children together."

Jesse chuckles. "It's going to be fine," he assures me. "I would never introduce you two if I thought it would go anything other than perfectly."

He pulls the car into a driveway and turns off the ignition. Only fifteen minutes away from his house, this one looks similar, even down to the loveseat and host of children's toys in the yard.

"Raine is spending the night at Zara's parents' place, and it's casual. No pretenses." Shifting in his seat, he turns to face me. "Give me your hands." I oblige and he clasps them together, bringing them to his lips to kiss.

Our eyes meet over the top of our joined hands, and the warmth he exudes from just a simple look settles my nerves.

Jesse and I have only been together for such a minuscule amount of time, but every time we're together he looks at me with an unspoken confidence and certainty that tells me he's all in.

He looks at me like he knows something about me that I don't. And whatever it is, it is the one thing that makes him want to stay.

And I want him to stay.

I'm not used to wanting anything for myself. I usually set my expectations very low, because I'm used to being disappointed. It's easier to be let down when your hopes aren't all that high to begin with.

But Jesse is above any expectation I ever had for myself. He's actually too good for anyone, but now that I've found him, there isn't a thing I won't do to keep him.

"Ready?" he asks.

"As I'll ever be."

He lets go of my hands and we both exit the car. Opening the back door, I pull out the box of gourmet donuts I bought for Zara. Jesse may have suggested they were her favorite, and there was no way I was going to show up empty handed anyway. Two birds, one stone.

Slipping his hand back in mine, Jesse leads us the short way to the house and up the porch steps. When we reach the front door, he doesn't bother knocking, showing just how close they really are.

"We're here," he announces, guiding me down a long hallway.

"In the kitchen," she shouts back.

We pass three closed doors as we walk through, with the end of the hallway opening up into a large living room, kitchen, and dining area combined.

Zara has her back to us, cooking something on the stove. Wearing black skinny-leg jeans, I notice she's taller than I expected—almost my height—and her dark brown hair falls in waves to the small of her back.

When she glances over her shoulder, her face is makeup free and her hazel eyes dart between the two of us with so much warmth that the minute amount of tension I was holding in my shoulders completely disappears.

I wasn't anticipating that she wouldn't like me, but it's the desperation in which I want her to, for Jesse, that makes me nervous.

"You guys are just on time," she says. She turns the burner down, whatever is on the stove now set to more of a simmer, and turns to face us. "And you must be Leo," she says.

I wave awkwardly. "In the flesh."

Her smile is still so wide, genuineness radiating off her. "I doubt he's spoken about me as much as he's spoken about you, but I'm Zara."

I extend my arm over the counter and she takes it. "He speaks about you and Raine plenty," I tell her.

Her gaze darts to him with a knowing smile; the man can't contain his feelings about anyone important to him to save his life.

When I release my hold on her, she takes a few steps to the fridge and opens it.

"Beer or wine?" she asks.

Jesse squeezes my hand and answers, "I'll take a beer and Leo will take a Coke."

Wordlessly, she takes out a bottle of each, turns to face us, and slides them over the kitchen island toward us. The fact that she doesn't balk or ask me questions about my drink of choice has me liking her even more. It's a probability that Jesse has already informed her about my parents, and my decision to drink as little as possible, but she takes it in stride, and I appreciate it.

Returning to the fridge, Zara pulls out a bottle of white wine, followed by a glass she must leave in there to keep cool.

"Everything Zara drinks has to be cold," Jesse explains.

"So no tea and coffee?" I ask her.

She opens the bottle of wine and fills the glass three quarters full. "Only if they're cold."

"For any particular reason?"

"I want to say something serious and deep." She lifts the glass to her lips for a quick sip. "But really I'm just so impatient and got sick of burning my tongue waiting for my drinks to cool down.

"Now what are you two waiting for? I've got my famous marinara sauce simmering." She points at me. "Which I know you eat because I checked with Jesse. And I've got freshly made pasta waiting to be boiled." She then shifts her attention to Jesse. "Pull a stool out for your man and tell me all the things."

I feel my cheeks heat at the attention as I take my seat, preparing for whatever interrogation is coming my way.

Sitting beside me, Jesse positions his stool so his body is

facing me as I face Zara. His legs are spread wide, both knees grazing my thigh, his hands free to touch me at any given time, something I've noticed he loves to do.

"How was Raine when you dropped her off?" Jesse asks Zara.

"The usual. She walks into their house and forgets I ever existed. It's quite offensive, actually, considering I gave birth to her."

If there is one thing I've noticed about Jesse, it's how much he loves talking about his daughter. And I love hearing it.

It's the perfect place to start the evening. "Tell me," I say, looking from Jesse to Zara. "What's Jesse like as a father?"

The question seems to put a smile on both their faces, obviously Raine being a favorite topic of conversation for both of them. Zara leaves the kitchen for a few minutes and comes back with a stack of photo journals I was not expecting to see.

Jesse grabs a few off the top and flicks quickly through the pages before handing them over to me.

Each photo of Jesse and Raine is like seeing Jesse for the first time. I thought the way he looks at me was enough to have me fall in love with him.

But with how he looks at Raine in these photos, I'm ready to marry him here and now.

The journals perfectly document Jesse and Zara's transformation from teenagers to adulthood, while Raine, who is the spitting image of Zara, continued to grow with them.

"These are beautiful," I tell them. "And such a good idea."

"Zara is behind all the creativity," Jesse informs me. "And I almost always forget to take photos."

They're a picture-perfect family, the love between the three of them emanating off the pages.

An unnamed emotion lodges itself on the inside of my rib cage. It feels a lot like jealousy, but I'm not sure what exactly I'm jealous of.

Of what they have together or the ease in which it comes? It feels like a standard that's almost impossible to measure up to. Like adding me to the mix might ruin their dynamic, and that makes me feel all sorts of ways.

Surprising myself, I look up at Zara. "Will you have any more kids?"

She's quick to shake her head. "I am one hundred percent content with the way things are. What about you?" she asks.

I glance at Jesse, who's sitting there, hanging on my every word. "Is there a right or wrong answer here?" I half-heartedly joke.

This isn't exactly the type of conversation you have with your boyfriend and his best friend/baby mama, but that isn't the reason I was thrown off.

I'd never really thought about it before, because I never saw myself in this situation. "I'm not opposed to it," I say honestly. I want to amend that I'm not opposed to it with Jesse, because I would be lying if I thought I could possibly feel this way about anybody else in the same lifetime.

It doesn't help that as a gay man I automatically default to not thinking about long-term relationships, marriage, and children. Just like straight people, I'm certain there are a large number of queer people who want those traditional things, but I'm even more certain that there is an even bigger number who think those things aren't an option for them.

I fall somewhere in between.

It's my turn to ask Jesse now. Privacy be damned, Zara very much obviously part of the conversation. "What about you?"

His hand now squeezes my thigh, his attention only on me. "I'll have kids with you."

My chest tightens and a blush creeps up my neck and onto my cheeks. Zara makes a gagging sound, just to tease us.

It's the levity I need, while Jesse just continues to hold my gaze, completely unfazed by the way he just stole the breath right out of my lungs.

When the words don't come, I grab a fistful of his shirt and drag him to me, melding his lips to mine. He doesn't hesitate to kiss me back, his hands on my neck, keeping us in place. The kiss deepens without a care in the world that this is Zara's kitchen or that she's our audience.

Every kiss with Jesse peels away another layer of the protection I try to keep around myself. It's always raw and vulnerable, and it's getting harder to keep my old walls up and my new feelings hidden. He turns the most mundane things into memories that will stay with me till the day I die.

With the simplest of words, he is changing me. Digging himself so deep beneath the surface, I don't know any other way to show him just how much I love whatever it is we're starting but to be touching him. All the time, in any way I can.

"Okay then," Zara says as we pull apart. "I guess I can get used to that."

I lean my forehead against Jesse's and smile at her words. I turn to look at her. "Does that mean I get to stay?"

Her eyes soften, the humor being replaced by adoration,

as she shifts her gaze to Jesse but answers me. "You get to stay."

"You are not shaving his hair," Jesse says firmly.

We're sitting in the living room now, done with dinner, the three of us talking effortlessly about everything and anything, including Zara's firm rule that ever since she became a hairdresser, all family members, which apparently now includes me, have to have their hair cut by her.

"I didn't say shave," she argues. "I said cut."

I'm quite indifferent to the idea, but even though I need a little trim, I know Jesse is fond of my curls. He often absentmindedly runs his hands through them when we're talking or lying in bed together.

"It's like an initiation." Zara animatedly jumps off the couch and grabs my arm. "Come on."

I don't really have time to argue, so I just let her lead me to a bathroom off the hallway and close the door.

"What are we doing in here?"

"Pissing Jesse off," she says casually, her eyes full of excitement.

"You do this a lot, don't you?"

She nods as she strides to the cabinet and begins pulling things out of her bathroom drawers. "Usually I'm trying to recruit Raine into helping me, but that takes a lot of bribing."

"I can be bribed," I say.

I catch Zara rolling her eyes. "Who do you think you're fooling? You're a mess for that man."

She isn't wrong, but I also enjoy riling Jesse up just as

much as the next person. He always wins, but if our first night was anything to go by, I occasionally have some pull.

"Let's shave my hair," I suggest.

"I wonder who he'll kill first," she says with a smile on her face.

As the night progressed, I began to see the layers that made up Zara. She was a mother and she was Jesse's best friend, but she was also a twenty-six-year-old woman who chose a different path for her life and was giving herself freedom to enjoy it wherever she could.

It's obvious she is the chaos and Jesse is the calm. They complement each other, and I'm certain their parenting and raising of Raine is exactly the same.

"I could probably suck his dick and save us both," I joke.

Zara squeals. "That's fucking brilliant."

She guides me to the edge of the bathtub and sits me down. "He's trying to be patient out there, but we're about five seconds from him storming in here."

"Hurry," I urge.

She puts a cape over my clothes and then grabs the cordless hair clippers, switches them on, and lets the loud rumble of the machine echo off the walls.

Just as she presses them to my head, Jesse barges in. Certain she's spurred on by his arrival, Zara glides the blade down the middle of my head, just as Jesse's eyes land on me.

"Zara," he warns.

Unperturbed, she just shrugs. "Don't be jealous. I can do yours right after."

Looking at me, Jesse shakes his head, watching Zara expertly shave my hair off. My curls land on the cape before they fall to the floor.

"You're never cutting his hair again," Jesse says, walking farther into the bathroom. "I'm going to make sure he goes somewhere else on purpose."

There's nothing but humor in his voice as he reaches for the clippers and pushes Zara aside. He continues to shave my head, as if he's the one who's been doing it all along. His touch is soft and gentle, and for some reason, that has heat racing up and down my spine.

When he tilts my head up to get a good look at me, he's gazing down at me with a reverence I hardly deserve.

I run my hand over my shorn head.

"You're still beautiful," he says.

"Holy fuck," Zara interrupts, clearly caught in our orbit once again. "I have never felt more single in my life."

She snatches the clippers off Jesse and hands him a brush that helps clean the hair off me. "I can't with all the googly eyes. You're both nauseating. Let's never hang out just the three of us ever again."

She glances at me while continuing to clean up around me. "Next time you want to do something"—she points at Jesse before taking the cape off me—"*he* is not allowed to come. Mr. Smooth Operator is ruining everything."

"Do you want to have a shower?" Jesse asks, completely ignoring Zara's rant.

"Oh no. No sex in this house." She shoves him out of the way and then moves my head in different angles, inspecting his work. "If I'm not getting any, neither are either of you."

"I simply asked if he wanted a shower," Jesse interjects. "Nobody said anything about sex."

"I've got eyes," she counters. "I'm surprised you're not fucking on the floor right now."

She darts out of the room quickly and returns with a

stand-up vacuum and hands it to me. "In this family you earn your keep."

She grabs Jesse's hands and begins dragging him out of the bathroom. "There're towels in the cabinets," she calls out. "Use whatever soap and shampoo is in the bathroom."

My smile is wide. Stupidly wide as I vacuum the bathroom and try to rid my clothes of any remainders of hair.

I find a towel, get naked, and jump in for a quick shower, still looking like a smiling fool.

In this family you earn your keep.

CHAPTER TEN

NOW

IF LEO and I had made any progress since our last therapy session, I had undoubtedly ruined it when I asked him to leave the house.

I shocked myself when the words left my mouth, and when his face fell, it took every ounce of strength I had not to change my mind. This wasn't just some verbal sparring between us, where you sling words back and forth in the heat of the moment.

My request was intentional. It was picking a side, and I have never done that before.

Despite the hurt I know I caused him, a little spark of hope resurged the next day when he walked back into the house, duffle in tow, and headed straight back to sleep in the guest room.

It's been a week since then, and now my car is idling in the driveway, waiting for Leo to come out so we can go to our therapy session together.

I'm not thrilled about the fact that he was driving under the influence, but I'd be lying if I said I'm not secretly enjoying that he is somewhat bound to the one spot.

I don't have to worry about him leaving to go drinking, I don't have to worry about him driving, and I don't have to worry about whether or not he's coming home.

The passenger side door opens and Leo slides inside.

"Hey," I greet.

"Hey."

He slams the door shut and I back us out of the driveway and start the short drive to Dr. Sosa's office.

We're about five minutes out when he asks, "Did you consider a time frame in which you want to commit to our sessions, like Dr. Sosa suggested?"

My heart deflates at his question. Did I think about her request? Yes. Often. Did I have an answer? Fuck no. I hate that we're even doing this, and he knows that.

"You mean did I come up with an end date for our marriage?" I snap back. "Did you?"

I brace myself for his answer, to hear how he's reduced our marriage to an arbitrary timeline that says nothing about how much we love each other or everything we've been through.

"I was hoping we could present a united front on this," he answers calmly. "It doesn't need to be another thing we can't agree on."

"It's not another thing we can't agree on," I say, trying to match his indifferent tone and failing. "It's the *only* thing we can't agree on."

That right there was a lie. There are probably a million things we couldn't agree on, but this is the only thing that matters. The outcome of this would change the trajectory of both of our lives, and I refuse to believe he is ready or really wants that.

When he asked me for a divorce, he was the most broken I've ever seen him. He was sitting on the kitchen floor after I picked him up from the bar—again—and just sobbing. Head buried in his hands, the tears didn't stop.

He cried over our daughter.

He cried over his lost job.

He just cried.

When we first started dating, Leo was in between jobs, and throughout the last seven years it has happened another few times. Because he left home so young, he's always worked just to stay afloat and has never really been given the financial freedom to go on his own journey of self-discovery.

I have always wanted to give him that. But when you add in life, weddings, mortgages, and the decision to start a family, you're once again dedicated to the nine-to-five grind and forced to pick and choose which one of your dreams gets to come true.

It was adulting. Sometimes it sucked, and sometimes you could maneuver all the shitty things you had to put up with and do and get it to work in your favor.

This is where our lives were before Lola. Our money was for the IVF process and all of Zara's medical expenses, and when Lola was born, Leo was going to quit his job, be a stay-at-home dad, and it would hopefully give him the time to find himself.

The excitement we all had for the next chapter was palpable in every aspect of our lives.

Now I think back to Leo crying on the kitchen floor, feeling like a failure, and begging me to give him a divorce.

I know my husband. I know he has insecurities and deep issues of inadequacy. I know he was trying to push me away because he thinks he's the weakest link in our family.

And if I truly believed that leaving me would guarantee him a pain-free and fulfilled life, I would've been the one to leave him a year ago. I would've handed him my bloodied heart on a silver platter—veins, arteries, and all—and begged him to go.

But this is not how life works, this is not how *our* life works.

Our life is me dangling a divorce in my husband's face with the hope that it might just make him want to stay.

It's fucked-up and more than likely going to blow up in my face.

But it's the only card I have left, the only thing I have that will keep him with me a little while longer.

"I don't want to fight with you," Leo says as I park in front of Dr. Sosa's office. "I just want us to be on the same page."

"Leo. Baby," I say with an exasperated breath. "We can't be on the same page when we're both reading a different fucking book."

AFTER A FIFTEEN-MINUTE WAIT, WE'RE FINALLY IN DR. SOSA'S office, sitting on opposite ends of the room, and I can feel the tension emanating off of him. He can't decide if he's mad or if I'm right, or maybe it's the fact that I'm right that makes him mad. Either way, he's sitting here with a chip on his shoulder and I'm over it.

"I picked Leo up from the police station the other night." I feel like the biggest tattletale, but I'm committed to the cause. "For drunk driving."

If she's surprised, she doesn't show it.

"Is that a first?" she asks him.

We both look at her, confused. "Is that the first time you

were driving under the influence or the first time you got caught?"

My lungs tighten in anticipation, waiting for his answer. The idea of him doing this on the regular never even crossed my mind.

He turns his body to face me. "It was the only time."

"Why did you do it?" Dr. Sosa asks.

Despite her navigating the direction of the session, Leo only talks to me.

"I told you I was visiting Lola," he starts. "Remember when we were buying furniture for Lola's room and I found that house-shaped toddler bed?"

"Yeah," I draw out, not sure how one is related to the other.

"You told me there was still at least eighteen months or more till she needed that bed, but I wanted her to have that one," he reminisces. "I remember calling the store and they told me there was an eight-month wait on the bed anyway. It was perfect," he adds. "So, I paid in full and they said they would call me when the bed came in."

The puzzle pieces start clicking together as he continues to explain. "I forgot I ordered it and they called." I watch his throat bob. "So here I am, sitting beside my daughter's grave, talking to a woman who's telling me how she has the same bed for her granddaughter and she knows just the place to refer me to for bed sheets."

Wet, green eyes dart between me and Dr. Sosa. "I lost it," he admits, hanging his head in shame. "I took myself to the bar and I drank. And drank. And drank."

"But why did you get in the car?" I find myself asking the question now that I know he wasn't intentionally trying to hurt himself. "You know you could've called me.

You could've called Gio," I amend, knowing he's not yet in a place to call me when he needs help.

"I didn't realize how much I'd drank till it was too late," he tells me. "And I thought if I could just get myself home, save myself from another lecture from Gio, then the next day would be better."

The three of us sit in silence, Leo and I not sure where to go from here. I'm grateful to get the bigger picture, but it doesn't change his recklessness and my concerns.

"What happened after you were arrested?" Dr. Sosa asks. "What were the consequences?"

"My license has been suspended for six months," he informs her. "I have a two-thousand-dollar fine to pay, plus the lawyer fees, and I was ordered to attend an outpatient rehab program. It's one day a week for twelve weeks."

"How do you feel about the outpatient rehab program?" she asks him.

With my hands clasped together and my chin to my chest, I wait for his answer. This is the exact moment where it all fell apart for us the other day.

I know he knows he has a problem, but I also know how hard it is for him to admit it. Because for him there is only one way to be an alcoholic, and that's like his parents. And he isn't them.

"I don't see the point," he says. "But considering I am currently jobless, one day of not being at home isn't going to kill me."

I hear the sarcasm, but I also hear the concession, and that's enough for me.

"That's good," Dr. Sosa praises. "I think you might actually find some benefit in it by the end of the twelve weeks. And you know you can always check in with me after those sessions, especially if you feel like they might become too much."

She doesn't elaborate on what "too much" actually means, but her offer to be there for him, even when we're not inside this room, gives me both hope and comfort.

"Before I forget." She twirls her pen between her fingers as she speaks. "I wanted to know if you two have managed to agree on a number of sessions you could do together, or for how long you may want to do them."

Our eyes meet, and dread settles in my stomach. I'm not ready to hear his answer. I'm not ready for this to be the beginning of the end.

"It's up to Jesse," he says, knocking the wind out of me.

My eyes widen. "The fuck it is."

"Why do you say that, Leo?" Dr. Sosa interjects.

"He wanted us to come to therapy," he says, shifting his gaze to hers. "He said he wouldn't agree to a divorce without therapy."

He thinks he's so clever trying to turn the tables on me. "If that's the case," I respond nonchalantly, "then I suggest we commit to a year of therapy."

"Are you kidding me?" he blurts out.

"You said it was up to me."

"Okay." Dr. Sosa puts her hands up in the air. "What if we stop there for a second. I have a follow-up question to ask you both.

"Jesse, is it safe to say reconciliation is an option for you?"

I want to roll my eyes, because the word feels so inadequate for what I want for us, but I nod anyway.

"And you, Leo?"

He's biting his cuticles, brows knitted together, thinking impossibly hard. I can't read him, but I'm desperate to hear his answer. Is there a way I can get through to him?

Is there a way I can make him want to fight for us or make him want to stay?

"I don't know," he answers, and I have to be grateful for his honesty. "I want to say yes." He meets my gaze. "But I don't even feel like we know one another anymore."

"Could you get to know one another again," she suggests. "Maybe—"

"I don't mean it like that," he cuts her off and shakes his head. "We're just not the same anymore. *I'm* not the same," he confesses. "I don't know how to be anything else but this." He gestures at himself, waving his hand up and down his body. "I don't know how to do anything but exist as this sad man."

I don't know how many times he needs to hear it, but it's worth repeating. "Leo, I don't care if you exist as this sad man for the rest of our lives."

"But I care," he shouts. "I don't think I want to change, but I don't want to make you live like this."

Whether he realizes it or not, this is the first time he's ever made mention of me and my feelings and that he cares about them.

It's dangerous, because I want to latch on to it like a lifeline.

"Why can't I make that decision for myself?" I ask. "Why can't I tell you what I can and can't handle? What I do and don't want?"

"Because we both know you'll stay," he says softly. "We both know your happiness comes last. It always has."

He isn't wrong, but I don't know why he sees it as a bad thing when I don't. When I'm taking care of the people I love, I'm happy; it's that simple.

"Jesse." Dr. Sosa's voice interrupts us, reminding me she's been here the whole time.

Without realizing it, my elbows are leaning on my knees, my hands are steepled together, and my shoulders are hunched forward. I tilt my head to look at her.

"I think it's important to acknowledge that Leo is concerned about you," she states, mirroring my earlier thoughts. "And, Leo, I also think it's important for you to trust that it's Jesse's responsibility to tell you when and if he's no longer happy in the marriage.

"Communication is so important, especially when everything is so fragile. I encourage couples to find a way to keep that line open with one another always. Otherwise, there is too much room for error, misunderstanding, and assumptions."

"He's not going to admit to being unhappy," Leo says at the same time as I say, "He won't believe me anyway."

"I think it would be great if you two worked on that." She resumes twirling her pen between her fingers. "Trusting the other enough to take what they say at face value is very important," she implores. "If you can think of one thing to say to each other before we end the session, it might help encourage you to keep it going when you leave."

She gives us both a soft, encouraging smile, and I try to rack my brain with something to say. Something he maybe doesn't already know but needs to hear.

But nothing comes.

The silence permeates the room and we both just sit here, feeling a little too raw and exposed in Dr. Sosa's presence.

She clears her throat. "I think that was a good session. But before you go, I would like to revisit your goals.

"There is no rush on your healing, but I would like to see you both comfortable with the direction of your relationship sooner rather than later. Deciding on a period of time also allows for you both to manage your expectations."

Leo and I look at each other, and I know neither one of us is going to offer up what she's asking.

"Can you suggest what would be a good amount of time to commit to this type of therapy?" I ask her.

"Absolutely," she confirms. "In these instances, I usually recommend once-a-week sessions for three months, each session being an hour long." She looks between us. "Would that work for both of you?"

Leo surprises me when he answers for us. "Yes. I think three months will work perfectly."

I simply nod, because if he's in, then so am I.

This officially ends the session and we all awkwardly meander around one another, standing and saying our goodbyes as we make our way to the exit.

It's such a surreal experience to sit in a stranger's office and find it to be the only way you can communicate with your significant other. But no matter the outcome, seeing Dr. Sosa these last few weeks has been the most honest conversations Leo and I have had in twelve months.

I don't know where we will be in another twelve months, but this makes me feel a lot more hopeful than him living at Gio's and barely talking to me.

We're sitting in my car now, and it dawns on me that there is one thing I do want to say. Words we haven't exchanged, words I still feel, stronger now than ever.

"I love you, Leo," I say. "No matter what you try to tell yourself or how unloveable you try to insist you are. I. Love. You."

I hear a soft sniffle followed by a wet laugh. "You say the sweetest things, but you've always been the dirtier fighter of the two of us."

"I'm not fighting dirty when it's the truth." In the spirit of honesty and generally pushing my luck, I add, "If the roles were reversed right now, would you fight for us? Would you let me go?"

A sigh of resignation fills the car, followed by his very telling silence. "Well?" I press.

"No," he says. "You know damn well I wouldn't let you go."

CHAPTER ELEVEN

leo

THEN

PUSHING the heavy glass door open, my eyes scan the hair salon, searching for Zara. When I spot her washing a client's hair by the row of basins, I wave.

Smiling, she raises a hand, gesturing for me to wait a minute. Instead of loitering in the waiting area, I duck back outside and go to the coffee shop next door and order us each a large caramel latte.

It wasn't surprising that we both like the same drink, because as it turns out, Zara and I have a lot more in common than Jesse and I do.

Jesse is a man of precision and purpose. We often joke that he is always the man with a plan. Zara and I are the complete opposite. We're fueled by feelings, both good and bad. We live in that single moment, and you'd have no idea what to expect with either of us because it could all change in a hot minute.

Which makes my visit to her workplace even more out of character. But being with Jesse is unlike anything I have ever done. It's stable. It's constant.

And I find myself wanting to make plans.

"Hey." Zara's voice comes up behind me just as my drink order is placed on the counter in front of us.

Carefully grabbing the two hot lattes, I turn to hand one to her and kiss her on the cheek. "How are you?"

"Good," she answers suspiciously. "And you?"

"You want to know why I'm here, don't you?"

"Well, it can't be an emergency with Jesse," she says. "You look too calm for that."

"I finished work early." I point to my head. "And I need a haircut."

Zara and I both work downtown. Her in a funky, hipster hair salon, and I'm two months into my new job as a bank teller for a popular financial chain.

She reaches for my hair and runs her fingers through my curls that have just started to grow back after she took the hair clippers to them. "You don't need a haircut, unless you're planning on letting me shave it again."

"I think Jesse will kill us both," I tell her. "But humor me anyway."

She doesn't balk at my request, and I appreciate it more than she knows. If it wasn't for the fact that I know she is the senior stylist who has free rein, I wouldn't bother her at work. It's been two months since I first met Zara, and the ease in which we both became a staple in one another's lives should've shocked me, but just like with Jesse, I'm smitten with her too.

"I just have to put some hair color on my client," she informs me. "But come inside, take a seat, and I can fit you in while we're waiting for theirs to set."

I grab her forearm before she leaves. "Thank you."

Nodding, she walks back inside and I follow. Zara

points to an empty station with the usual mounted mirror and cabinet setup. "Have a seat here."

I place my drink, wallet, and cell phone down in front of me and take my seat.

Five minutes later, Zara is back. She wraps the black cape around me and then places her hands on my shoulders and squeezes comfortingly.

"What's going on?" she asks.

I chew on the corner of my mouth before answering, "I'm meeting Raine this weekend."

Her body slumps imperceptibly, and I feel a sliver of guilt for making her worry.

"I know," she says. "Jesse organized it with me."

I know all that, and that isn't really the reason I'm here. "I don't know if he told you, but he's been busting my balls to meet her ever since you and I met."

"And you keep putting it off."

"I don't want to fuck this up," I say truthfully. "It almost feels too good to be true, and I know nothing about kids."

Zara reaches for a water spray and a comb from a nearby caddy and starts wetting and combing my hair. "Firstly," she starts. "She's ten and is easily unimpressed, so don't take it personally. Secondly, you can't fuck it up."

"Anything is possible," I say.

"Listen." She switches out the spray for scissors and starts trimming my hair. "She's exactly like Jesse. She looks like I pressed copy and paste on myself, but her whole personality is him."

The thought of a mini Jesse makes me smile.

"She's kind and funny and compassionate. Stubborn as hell or really determined, it's yet to be decided," she says with a soft chuckle. "She'll love you. The exact same way he does."

My eyes widen at her indirect admission. "What? Are you going to tell me he doesn't?" she asks.

"He hasn't said anything," I argue weakly.

"I'm sure he doesn't want to scare the fuck out of you," she admits. "He knows it overwhelms you how fast this is all moving. But, honestly, who cares if it's different or too soon? It just is, so enjoy it."

"You're so full of wisdom," I say sarcastically. "Anything you would care to share with the class?"

"I'm just saying, the man asks you to marry him on the daily. He's committed, and I don't see that changing. Don't overcomplicate something that's staring you in the face."

I know she's right, and I'm doing my very best to lean into it. But it feels too good to be true. Good things happened when you worked hard, and I'd done nothing to earn Jesse Hunt or the family that came with him.

"And you're okay with me meeting Raine?"

At this she rolls her eyes. "You know how Jesse and I are when it comes to Raine. Every stone is turned before we agree on something."

"So, I'm something you both agree on?" I say with a smile, hoping for levity.

She raises a hand. "No, I will not indulge in your need for praise."

I laugh. "I am not that bad."

"You're a proper slut for it."

"I am not."

"I've seen your face when Jesse compliments you."

"Well..." I smirk. "It's Jesse. And it is *very* different."

She dramatically places her hands over her ears and squints her eyes closed. "I don't want to hear about your kinks with Jesse. Hard pass. Thank you."

Returning the scissors and the comb to her caddy, she

grabs her duster brush and cleans any excess hair off my face, ears, and neck.

"Let's wash your hair." She guides me to the basin and then goes to check on her client before returning. "If it helps," she says, diving straight back into our conversation, "Raine is very excited to meet you."

"She is?"

"Jesse talks about you all the time to her." I feel my chest tighten as she continues. "They're the best of friends."

"Did you ever wish you could've made it work with Jesse?" I blurt out, grateful she's behind me and I can't see her face as she answers.

"Like romantically?"

"I guess."

"God, no," she exclaims. "Before we'd even seen the pink lines on the pregnancy test, Jesse and I knew it was not going to happen.

"And I don't ever feel like Raine is missing out on anything because we're not romantically involved," she explains. "We're happy people. Happy parents. And that counts for so much more than whether or not we're married."

She's one hundred percent right. I think of my own parents and my own upbringing; they weren't happy people nor were they happy parents. But, for some reason, society still gives them both a gold star for staying married.

"I think what you two have is perfect," I confess. "It kind of makes me a little intimidated." I take advantage of the fact neither of us are looking at each other and continue. "It's the perfect setup and it feels like such a privilege to be allowed to be part of that."

When Zara switches off the water and towel dries my

hair in silence, I'm convinced I've said something wrong or overstepped my boundaries. But when I catch her walking around the row of basins in my periphery to stand in front of me, I manage to pull myself upright, my spine straighter.

"We want you there." She places her hands on her hips and smiles. "Now, just don't fuck it up."

CHAPTER TWELVE

leo

NOW

THE KNOCK at the door surprises me. It's the middle of the day and everybody I know is either working or at school. Climbing off the couch, I reluctantly drag my feet and swing open the door.

I was anticipating someone selling Girl Scout cookies, maybe even someone trying to convert me to a new religion. What I wasn't anticipating was Zara.

She stares at me expectantly as my gaze takes her in. She's dressed in nothing but yoga pants and a sweater, her long brown hair haphazardly tied at the top of her head, and her face makeup free.

Her hazel eyes are filled with apprehension, the way she worries her lip even more proof she's nervous about being here.

"Is everything okay?" I manage to ask, realizing for a single moment that her visit might have nothing to do with me at all. "Jesse? Raine? Are they okay?"

Nodding, she raises a familiar bag into the air. "Need a haircut?"

It was our thing.

I had unintentionally started a tradition that would be the very basis of my relationship with Zara. Over the years, we've argued, we've cried, and we've laughed. We've experienced a myriad of emotions together that would all come to a head every time I sat down and had Zara cut my hair. It's our version of therapy, something that isn't always about Jesse or Raine, but where we end up almost always talking about them anyway.

In the past it had made everything feel better. It made everything feel whole.

I feel my tongue thicken inside my mouth, the words stuck, the emotions holding them hostage.

On instinct, I run my hands through my hair. It's a mess, and I know as much as Zara does that I've barely paid any attention to it since Lola died.

With her standing in front of me, a part of me has to wonder if my inability to cut my hair was a subconscious decision. My mind tying me to Zara and everything we've shared, when every other part of me has just wanted to get away.

"Come in," I manage to say, my voice thick and unused.

I open the door wider, inviting her in. She knows her way around this house like the back of her hand, but she just stands there.

"Do you want a drink or anything?" I ask her as I close the door.

She shakes her head stiffly, and I hate that I make her feel like that.

"Zara." I find the courage to say her name as I step closer, standing directly in front of her. "Did Jesse send you to check on me? Because you don't have to do that."

Her eyes fill with tears. "Where do you want me to set up?"

"Wait." I place my hand on hers. It feels so hypocritical to ask her what's wrong and to ask her to even consider telling me how she's feeling, but the words come out anyway. "Sit down and talk to me first."

Pulling her to the couch, I drag her down to sit on one end while I sit on the other. I don't know which one of us started avoiding the other first but, eventually, too many months had passed and too many things could no longer be said.

"I'm sorry Jesse asked you to leave the house the other day," she blurts out.

"What? No," I say incredulously, not expecting or needing what she's offering. "You have nothing to apologize for. And truth be told, I'm surprised he didn't ask me earlier."

I bring my legs up to my chest, wrap my arms around myself, and rest my chin on top of my knees. "I haven't made it easy for you or Raine to be here." Admitting that out loud makes me feel like a piece of shit, but she's here and it feels like it's time for truths.

"You and Jesse have held down the fort for a very long time, especially with Raine." I chance looking at her. "And I know it hasn't been easy for you—"

"Stop," she says, cutting me off and scooting closer. "There is not a single person that any of this has been easy on."

Zara stands up and shakes her hands out, almost like she's trying to rid her body of something.

"Can we cut your hair?" she asks. "This face-to-face shit isn't working for me."

I chuckle, and it surprises me. "Yeah. Where do you want to set up?"

"Outside is nice," she suggests. "And you know how much Jesse loves flyaway hairs in the yard."

Because we've done this a million times before, Zara picks up her bag and I head straight outside to grab the one chair Jesse allows us to use for haircuts. We meet on the patio where she's got her essentials set up, and she combs her way through my hair.

"You could've had someone else cut it," she says.

"I know."

"For what it's worth, I'm kind of glad nobody else touched it."

We sit in silence, reading between the lines, admitting, to ourselves at least, just how much we missed each other.

"What's the real reason you came over?" I ask. "Because we both know it wasn't to apologize for something you have no business apologizing for."

"I did come over for that."

"Okay," I concede. "But what *else* did you come over for?"

I hear her sharp inhale, almost like she's trying to find the courage to answer my question. "I'm worried about Jesse," she says. "I have always done my very best to stay out of your relationship, but sometimes the lines blur and—"

"Zara," I cut her off. "I can handle it. Just spit it out."

Her hands stop touching my head. "But can you? Handle it, I mean. Because I'm watching my best friend drown trying to keep you afloat."

Instantly my eyes close and my head falls in shame at her words. She tries quickly to retreat. "Leo, I'm sorry."

But I put up a hand, silencing her. She walks around me, and when I feel hands on my knees, I open my eyes and find her crouching down in front of me, her eyes glassy and apologetic.

"I shouldn't have said it like that," she says. She grabs my hands and squeezes. "I'm worried about Jesse, Leo. I'm worried that he's been taking care of us all for far too long. And I just want to know who's taking care of him."

Unbeknownst to Zara, I had placed that responsibility on her. "I thought you were," I tell her.

Her face blanches, and I see the second she no longer cares about hurting my feelings. "So what, you just wash your hands of him, just like that?"

"That's not what I said," I say sternly. "You asked who was taking care of him and I answered."

"And just out of curiosity, are you going to step up any time soon?"

I didn't have an answer for her. What I want to do and what I'm capable of are two very different things.

"Are you going to truly leave him?" Her voice cracks.

She's still crouched down in front of me, her body language not indifferent or uncomfortable. I don't know why that matters to me, but it offers enough of a safety net for me to try and explain to her exactly how I feel.

"I don't know," I tell her. "You're asking me if I'm going to step up and take care of him, and I think not feeling obligated to take care of me would be doing exactly that."

"Honestly, you're insufferable." She pushes off me and stands, raising her hands in the air in frustration. "You think losing you is what he needs? After everything you've both lost, you think losing *you* will make it better?"

"In time," I say confidently. "I can see the better life he'll have with you and Raine. I can see the better life he'll have with his family that isn't so beaten down and broken."

"Why do you say things like that?"

"Like what?"

She's back down crouching in front of me. "You say *his* family like you're not a part of that." I can see the heartbreak in her eyes as she continues. "Like you're not my best friend just as much as he is. As if you're not Raine's father just as much as he is. Like being Jesse's husband isn't enough to make you part of this family."

As I sit there with wet hair and a hairdresser's cape on, she delivers blow after blow, reality check after reality check.

"How do you do it?" I ask her. "How do you and Jesse just get up every day and do the things that need to be done?"

I don't, for even a second, doubt their love for Lola, but I truly want to know why they could and I couldn't.

"It just looks different," she says. "I cry every day. I cried the day after and I'm still crying fifteen months later."

She turns to look at the pool behind her, and I catch the movement of her hands that suggests she's wiping her eyes. "Jesse swims. Some days when you weren't here, Raine would call me and tell me he'd been in the pool, swimming laps for hours. She didn't know whether to leave him alone or tell him to come out."

"And then there's Raine."

She doesn't look back at me this time, and I feel the pain she holds for her daughter. Pain I know I've caused.

"She's too much like Jesse," she continues. "She bottles it all up to protect us all. It'll be years before I know how deep this loss is for her."

"I'm sorry," I say, my voice thick with emotion.

"No." She shakes her head and looks at me over her shoulder, tears streaming freely down her face. "You don't get to wear that one alone."

She shifts her gaze back to the pool. "But I do need you to be around when she crumbles. Jesse and I both do."

"I never wanted any of this, you know?" I hear my thoughts tumble out of my mouth before I have the chance to take them back. "Marriage, kids. I didn't care for any of it till I met Jesse. And then you and Raine." I wring my hands together underneath the cape. "Having you both in my life was like being accepted into the cool club.

"I finally felt like I belonged somewhere and I could stop chasing my tail," I admit. "Add in Jesse, and I felt invincible. Like we could have it all."

I know we're both lost in thought, remembering that day. How we went from having it all to losing it all in the very same breath.

"Did Jesse ever tell you before you got pregnant we found out I was sterile?"

"No." Her eyes widen as she walks back in my direction. "I know it seems like we tell each other everything, but he didn't tell me that." She raises a finger in the air as she walks past me and back into position to cut my hair. "If I remember correctly, it was you who told me you two weren't going to find out which sperm was used in the insemination or which fertilized. So I assumed that meant both were viable."

Zara resumes combing and wetting my hair, the conversation between us still heavy, but it's lost the tension.

"It blew my mind that I never wanted kids, then when I decided otherwise, I couldn't have them. I anticipated issues with adoption and fostering and surrogacy as a gay man, but not once... not ever did I expect to be told I was sterile. And it became one more thing I couldn't do."

"Does Jesse know how you feel about this?" she asks.

"He does. Before we lost Lola, I told him everything."

My chest longs for the ease of those days with him, when I wasn't riddled with self-doubt and loathing.

"You know there's nothing you could say now that would make him turn his back on you, right?"

It isn't what I'm afraid of. I know he isn't going anywhere, but I don't want to hurt him with the thoughts that make me hurt. They're untrue and they are ugly, but the thing about insecurities and a childhood riddled with neglect is there is no rationale.

There is no such thing as common sense and logic. It's just pain, heartache, and no coping skills.

It doesn't matter whether I had a biological stake in Lola, she was still mine just like Raine, but my brain continues to tell me since there is no biological attachment, there is no place for me.

The family was Zara and Jesse and Raine and Lola. They didn't need me. And when Lola died, I felt that right down to the marrow of my bones.

But here I am, sitting here getting my hair cut by a woman who would die for me if she needed to. I have a husband who loves me and a daughter who calls me Papa because she loves me like I'm her own.

I'm worth something to them; I just need to work out how to believe it too.

"I know that," I finally manage to say. "But you were right. Who is taking care of him? Who is going to catch him when he falls?"

"It could be me," Zara answers. "But it should be you."

jesse

NOW

KICKING off my shoes at the front door, I walk straight to the laundry room to get out of my grease-stained clothes. I throw them in the wash and head to my room to shower.

I'm momentarily stunned when I see Leo asleep in our bed. As I walk closer to him, I notice his hair, cut and styled in a way I haven't seen for so long. The change brings me to my knees beside the bed.

Fingers from one of my hands skate down the side of his face and the other hand plays with his shorter, neater curls.

His eyes eventually flutter open and I watch his facial expressions change as he processes my presence. He takes in the room and then the bed.

"I sleep in here sometimes," he confesses. "When you're not home."

"This is your bed too," I remind him. "You got a haircut?"

As if I've just reminded him, he runs his hand over the top of his head.

"Zara came over and did it for me." His eyes nervously search my face. I don't know what he's looking for or what he'll find, but I know my heart is beating wildly inside my chest at his revelation.

So much so that I have absolutely no idea how to process the information.

What does it mean? What doesn't it mean? Why did he let his guard down for her and not me?

I clear my throat. "I'm going to take a shower."

Reluctantly, I leave him and try to straighten myself and my thoughts out in the shower. Some days felt like we were moving forward, and that's exactly what this, with Zara, is, but for some reason it hurts. It makes me feel like I don't actually know what forward for us truly looks like.

I go through the motions, washing my body and hair on autopilot, my mind a million miles away. When I get out of the shower and walk back into our bedroom, I hate myself for being relieved that he isn't still lying there in our bed, with his fresh haircut, looking like hope and heartache.

In an uncharacteristic move, I get myself dressed in jeans and a shirt and decide I need to leave the house.

"You're leaving?" Leo asks as soon as I exit our room and enter the living area. I realize quickly my clothes are the tip-off.

"Yeah, I have somewhere to be," I lie.

"Oh, okay." It's then I notice the boiling pot and fry pan on the stove. I shift my gaze just in time to catch the sad, rejected look on his face, and the irony of it all makes my blood boil.

"Fuck this," I mutter.

I don't dare look at him, because he's still Leo and I'm still me, and if I hold out even a second longer, I'll stay so I don't have to see the same look on his face that I know I've had on mine for *months.*

I don't make a huge production of leaving the house. I don't say a word. Not even a goodbye.

When I get in my car, I fuck around with the display screen and call Zara.

"Hey, Dad," Raine answers after three rings, and her voice immediately calms me down. "Hey, babe, how are you?"

"Good. I'm just waiting for Mom to get out of the shower."

"How is she today?" I ask.

"Ah, she's good?" Raine answers, but it sounds more like she's questioning my question. "Did something happen?"

"No," I lie. "I was just checking in and making sure everything was set for you to come over this weekend. I couldn't remember if you were coming over Thursday or Friday night."

"Oh, about that," she says, her voice cautious. "I'm not going to come this weekend."

"What? Why?" I know the answer, it's been the same song and dance, or at least a variation of it, since Leo returned home.

When Lola died, just like the rest of us, Raine was devastated. But my daughter was too like me, and she put on her mask and played the role of perfectly fine better than I ever could.

Zara and I told the school about our circumstances and asked them to advise us if they noticed any changes in her behavior or her school work and to let us know if anything out of the ordinary happened... A phone call from them never came.

But just as I'm starting to feel my impatience increase as of late, I'm certain she has to be feeling the same way too. I imagine her to be annoyed by all the changes. All the back and forth, all the hot and cold.

"I'm sorry you don't feel comfortable at our place anymore," I tell her.

"Dad." She sighs. "It's not like that. Things are just different. I'm getting busier with spring break coming up."

I swallow her lie, because who am I to pull her up on her avoidance tactics when I just left my own house for the same reason?

"Do you have any free time in between your plans for me to come over on the weekend? It can be just the two of us, or Mom can join us if she doesn't have plans."

"I don't have plans," Zara's voice comes through. "Come over whenever you want."

There's some muffled discussion on the other end before Raine says goodbye and hands the phone to Zara.

"You're off loudspeaker now," she informs me knowingly.

"You cut Leo's hair."

"I did," she draws out.

When nothing but silence follows, I huff. "Is that really all you're going to give me?"

"You've both been going to therapy and you mentioned there was some progress," she says. "I wanted to see for myself if it was true."

"And?"

I don't know why I wait with bated breath or even why her approval matters, but I need someone to tell me I'm not making things up for the sake of holding on to something that is no longer within my reach.

"He's different," she says softly. "Still him, still sad, but he listened when I spoke to him, and he told me things he's never mentioned before."

I don't ask her what he told her, because I'm not ready to hear it. I'm not ready to acknowledge that I may no longer be the person he turns to.

"You know he still loves you, right?"

"Fuuuck. No, I don't know anything," I shout, pounding my fist on the steering wheel. "I'm just so fucking mad right now. I saw him this evening, sleeping in our bed with his haircut that means so much, and I'm supposed to feel something other than all this rage."

"What are you doing now?" she asks. "Do you want to come over?"

"No. I'm just aimlessly driving around. I think I'm going to find a bar and park myself on a stool for a couple of hours."

"Jess." It's a warning almost, because she knows as well as I do, I don't drink more than a beer at dinner, if that. "Be careful, okay? And if you drink as much as I'm expecting you to, please call me to pick you up."

"I'll get an Uber."

"I'll check your locations."

This makes me huff out a laugh. "I'll call you tomorrow." Before I hang up, I remember one more thing. "Thank you for today," I tell her. "He probably doesn't even realize how much he needed that."

"Don't kid yourself, Jess. I think you needed it more."

———

THE BAR IS PRETTY MUCH EMPTY AND I'M ON MY FOURTH WHISKEY when a tall, slim man with a buzz cut, a beard, and a familiar face appears behind the bar. I'm not intoxicated enough that I can't walk or talk, but I can feel the buzz loosen my inhibitions just enough.

As if he can feel me staring, his gaze lands on me and recognition settles on his features. "Ahh, I remember you." He starts walking toward me. "If you're in here, does that mean there's still trouble in paradise?"

My jaw clenches at the fact that this stranger and I have met twice and both times he's alluded to knowing more about Leo than he should.

He glances at my drink and I watch him pour another and push it across to me. "Calm down, big boy. I'm just messing with you."

Instead of taking it, I slide it back to him, refusing to accept his peace offering.

"Come on, it's on the house," he persists, trying to pass it back to me. When I decline a second time, he grabs the tumbler and raises it to his lips, throwing the amber liquid down his throat in one gulp.

He slams the glass against the bar top and keeps his eyes on mine for a few seconds too long before returning to restocking drinks and serving other customers. It's unnerving being around him, knowing that he is just another person who isn't me that Leo has confided in.

I debate leaving and calling it quits for the night, but the bartender returns, a thoughtful look crossing his features. "Is he okay?" he asks.

Confused as hell, I shake my head at him. "What are you talking about?"

"Leo," he says. "He hasn't been by since that night you picked him up, and I'm hoping it's for a good reason and nothing's happened to him."

I hate the way his concern both dissipates and ignites my anger. It's proof that Leo didn't come here the night he got drunk and drove, but it's also obvious that this man *knows* Leo. "He's fine," I answer curtly.

"Well, if he's fine, why are you here?"

Isn't that the million-dollar question, and also, what the fuck is up with this guy?

"If you're expecting me to pour my heart out to you, you've got the wrong guy."

"I'm not expecting anything." He leans in on his forearms and moves into my personal space. "I just don't often get to see who my regulars are always talking about in the flesh."

"Are you kidding right now?" He's riling me up on purpose, wanting me to ask about Leo, and I'm one hundred percent taking the bait. "He isn't one of your regulars," I spit out. "He isn't one of your anything."

I'm being petty and territorial and he's enjoying it.

"Relax," he says nonchalantly. "No need to get so worked up. I know he's yours and I don't really shit where I eat, if you know what I mean."

Wordlessly, he pours me another drink, and this time I take it and don't even bother to sip on it slowly. It burns the whole way down.

I slide the empty glass to him and he pours me another finger, and I drink it just as quickly.

The looseness my body was feeling from earlier has just turned into a mountain of unmatched emotions lodged inside my chest. I came here to get out of my house and clear my head, but I'm leaving feeling even more helpless and clueless than before.

I throw a few bills out in front of me and climb off the stool. The rush throws me off balance and I quickly hold on to the bar to catch myself.

"Wait," the bartender calls out. "You're not driving are you?"

I'm not, but after what I just went through with Leo, I

could find it in me to be grateful he asked.

I shake my head. "No, I'll book an Uber."

He nods, satisfied with my response.

I pat myself down, checking I have my keys, wallet, and cell. As I turn to leave, I hear him call my name.

"Jesse."

When I half turn my body to look at him, my face must show my surprise.

"Yeah, so I know your name," he says unapologetically. "He talked about you a lot. And I'm not really one to get into a stranger's business."

At this I raise my eyebrows, because that's not really how I remember it and he knows it.

"Okay, fine, whatever." He rubs the back of his neck. "I'm just saying, if you guys can fix it, it'll be worth it."

I'm not going to argue with a stranger about the semantics of "whether we could fix it" versus "what the fuck do you think I've been trying to do," but I've definitely hit my limit for the night and I just need to get home.

There's nothing left for me here besides the bottom of an empty glass, and I'm not going to find what I'm looking for there.

Without a goodbye, I exit the bar and eventually find my ride. It's a short drive, where even small talk with the driver is too much for me to muster. I text Zara to let her know I'm home as I walk through the front door, and instead of making my way to my room, I take my shoes and socks off in the living room and find myself standing outside what's now Leo's bedroom.

The door is ajar, so I push it open and lean on the wooden frame. The low light of a bedside lamp fills the room. His arms and legs peek out of the blankets just enough for me to guess he's wearing nothing more than briefs.

My own body stirs at the thought, but the residual anger of the evening still has my blood at a low simmer. He shifts against the sheets and, as if he can feel me standing there watching him, his head turns and his eyes slowly open, trying to adjust to the light.

His tired gaze gives nothing away as he stares at me expectantly.

"I thought you said you sleep in our bed when I'm not home," I say, almost accusingly. "I guess you won't do it now I know, because then I would think you actually gave a shit about us, right?"

"Jesse," he breathes out. He sits himself up, exposing his naked chest. "You know that's not true."

"Do I?" I scoff, pushing myself off the door and stepping into the room. "Because it kinda feels like everybody else fucking knows that you give a fuck except me." My eyes sting and my voice cracks. "You want to tell everybody else but me you still love me and expect me to keep fucking going?"

"Jesse," he says with a bit more urgency. "Listen."

"I listen," I shout, moving even closer to the bed. "I'm here waiting and ready all the fucking time and you give me crumbs, at best."

He rises to his knees now, his body wanting to reach for me, but he can feel the anger radiating off me and he's torn.

"Jesse," he repeats, the tremble in his voice unmissable.

I can hear the words before he says them and I shake my head, vehemently. Only a breath apart now, I roughly grab his face as my heart bleeds between us. "Don't you dare say it now."

Leo opens his mouth, but before the three words I need

the most eviscerate me, I slam my mouth to his, silencing him.

The kiss is hard and bruising, nothing but teeth and tongues, but even in my anger I don't miss the perfection of how his mouth fits against mine.

My hand moves down to his throat, and a small squeeze has Leo's lips faltering and the sexiest whimper leaving his mouth. The thrumming of his pulse underneath my fingers makes my cock thicken.

"Do you know how hard it is to have you so close but still so out of my reach?" I murmur against his lips.

My mouth moves from his and finds that sweet spot on the curve of his neck. He hisses as I alternate between sucking on his skin, hard, and soothing the sting with my tongue. I want to mark him everywhere. I want to bruise his body with my mouth. I want him to look in the mirror every day for the next week and know there is no escaping me.

Stepping away from the bed, I take him in, my eyes darting around the expanse of his bare skin. The way he sits on his haunches, dick straining against his underwear, my own cock leaks at the sight of him. The way his eyes blaze with heat, the way the mark I left on him is already blooming into the most beautiful blemish.

I tug my t-shirt over my head and rid myself of my pants and underwear. Leo licks his lips as his gaze travels down my body and stops at my erection. His own hand travels down to his briefs, squeezing his cock.

"How do you want me?" he asks, sitting there, looking at me, everything about his body willing and wanting.

I want him to be at my mercy, to feel just how wound up I am over him, because Jesus fucking Christ I am losing my mind trying to save us. I'm over here trying to be a

Goddamn martyr, but tonight I want nothing more than to succumb to my rage and take him with me.

"Get naked," I command. "All fours, ass up."

He doesn't waste a single second, positioning himself perfectly at the edge of the mattress. Head down, back bowed, ass up and ready for the taking. He is fucking beautiful, and in this moment I hate him for it. I hate him for being everything I love and everything that hurts.

Leaning over him, I run one lone finger down his spine and then down his crease, enjoying the eruption of goosebumps all over his skin.

"You're always so fucking pretty," I spit out, slapping his ass at the same time.

He glances over his shoulder. "Only for you."

His words make me feel unhinged and desperate. My cock aches to be inside him. To own him, to claim him. To remind him his body is nothing if it isn't mine.

Reaching between his spread legs, I grab his stiff length, stroking and squeezing, working my fingers over his wet slit and then repeating it all over again.

Determined to keep his eyes on me, I feel Leo's gaze follow my movements as I lower my mouth to one of his ass cheeks. I continue to jerk him off while my mouth latches on to him. Just like his neck, I mark him, sucking and licking his smooth flesh.

Once.

Twice.

Three times.

Rearing my head back, I take in his bruise-decorated ass, and my body thrums with a possessiveness I didn't know I could feel swimming in my veins.

Releasing my hold on his cock, I stretch out one of his cheeks, giving myself the perfect view of his hole. With my fingers coated in his sticky arousal, I repeatedly circle the puckered skin, pressing against it every so often.

Needing more, I lower my mouth to his opening, Leo's groan matching my own when I taste his arousal. I fuck his hole with my tongue, enjoying the way his body shudders and squirms beneath me.

When he's covered in my saliva, I roughly slide one finger inside. Thrusting, I purposefully avoid hitting his prostate, only wanting him to feel the stretch and burn of my fingers.

I shift my focus back to Leo's face, finding it flushed, his eyes alight with lust.

"More," he says, holding my stare.

Watching him, I push in another finger, enjoying the way he inhales, almost searching for air, as I widen him farther.

"More," he repeats, this time his voice hoarse.

I add another, but this time my attention is torn between his face and the way his body equally stretches and clenches around my fingers.

"Fuck. Jesse," he groans as I continue to push in and out of him. "I need your cock. Please."

There is no slow and sensual lead up as I slide my fingers out of him. I lick him one more time, spearing and circling his opening, before spitting on his hole, wanting to make it as wet as possible.

With my hold on him still tight, I stand at my full height and hold my throbbing cock with the tip to his center. Pre-cum pools at the crown and I smear it all over his hole, making the perfect mess.

Lining myself up, I press into him and watch the tip of my cock disappear inside him.

"Please," he begs. "Fuck me."

He's nowhere near ready for me. I gave him the laziest amount of preparation considering how long it's been since I've been inside him, but this is where we both are. We can't reach the pleasure without pushing through the pain.

I plunge myself inside him, and I feel, all the way down to my balls, the hoarse cry that rips out of Leo's throat.

"Fuck, you hurt so good," I grind out.

His body strangles my cock as my hips buck in and out of him.

Every thrust is heaven and hell.

In and out.

Everything I loved. Everything I lost.

Wrapping my arms around his chest, I bring his body up to me, his back now against my front.

The angle of my cock is deeper, harsher.

His head cants toward me and I capture his mouth in a furious kiss. Ravaging him. Hating him.

We're both on the edge, the fall into the aftermath inevitable.

"I hate you for making me feel like this," I grit out.

"I know," he cries. "Fuck. Baby, I know."

Pushing him back down to the bed, I grip his hips and fuck him mercilessly. There is no romance, no heart, no Leo and Jesse as I pound into my husband.

I reach for Leo's cock and he swats my hand away. "Just you," he breathes out. "Only for you."

His self-denial ignites a familiar searing heat through my veins and in my bones. I chase that one good feeling. Relentlessly.

Over and over and over until there's nothing left.

My orgasm ricochets through me, weakening my limbs, my muscles, my resolve.

My cum fills Leo, and I'm not ready to let it slip out.

Letting myself sag on top of him, I wait for my breathing to even out before making my move.

"Jesse," he breathes out.

"Not yet," I warn.

Slowly, I pick myself up off him and watch as I reluctantly pull my cock out of his body.

Strings of my arousal follow me, and I just swipe at them with my fingers and push them back inside of him.

There's satisfaction in the whimper that leaves his mouth.

I make an absolute mess of him, mark him, keep some part of me visible on him for as long as I possibly can.

Because that's all I have to give.

I'm almost certain he's lost the rest of me.

CHAPTER FOURTEEN

NOW

"IS THAT A HICKEY ON YOUR NECK?" Gio asks.

I reach for the almost faded bruise but ignore his question.

"Leo," he says, as if I didn't hear him. "I know you're not out there sleeping with anyone else."

"What do you mean?" I deadpan. "Don't I look like the type of guy who will cheat on his husband while their marriage is in crisis?"

"Okayyy then," Gio says more to himself than me. "Anything you want to talk about?"

"I need a job," I say, moving away from anything remotely close to hickey talk.

Gio and I are sitting across from one another at the coffee shop right next door to the physical therapy clinic he owns. We've already finished lunch and now we're just sipping our coffees. Like the good best friend he is, Gio asks me almost daily to join him for lunch, making sure I know that I have someone to turn to and some place to land, if I need.

And so many times I did, and Gio is always there.

I owed the people in my life more than I could ever repay, especially Gio and especially in the last twelve months.

So, when the mornings weren't too hard, I pushed myself to leave the house and see him. It isn't easy and I'm not really good at it, but between the unemployment, the DUI charges, and everything else in between, I'm coming to terms with the fact that things need to change.

I need to change.

"A job is great, but what about that hickey?" Gio persists.

I shrug nonchalantly. "Don't act so surprised. Who do you think I got it from?"

"Did you have sex?" he asks.

There is nothing but genuine curiosity in his question, but it's too difficult for me to answer, because Jesse and I didn't just have sex.

What happened that night felt almost sacred. Like a secret. In seven years I had never seen my husband unravel the way he did that night.

I've seen him happy, I've seen him angry, I've seen him sad, I've seen him grieving. I've seen him in all the ways one could see the one they love, but I had never seen him spiral.

And I wasn't prepared for the way it made me feel.

He is my rock, and my rock is cracking, and it's all my fault.

"Earth to Leo." Gio waves his hands in front of my face. "Where'd you go just now?"

"Nowhere," I answer absently. "Now. A job. You got any ideas?"

This time Gio raises a knowing eyebrow at me but

follows the conversation change nonetheless. "For the millionth time," he says, "you could just work with me."

"You mean *for* you," I argue.

"Is it that big of a deal?"

"No." I reach for my large coffee that sits between us. "But you're a physical therapist and there is absolutely nothing in your line of work that I am remotely qualified for."

"And?"

"And," I repeat. "I know you. You'll end up creating a whole new role that is completely irrelevant, just so I can work there. It's too much."

"It doesn't have to be permanent," he presses. "Just until you find something that suits you right now."

I don't miss his word choice; I know it's deliberate and I'm grateful.

Before Lola died I was working as an emergency dispatcher. It was, like most of my jobs, one I fell into by accident. I had never envisioned myself in that role or even thought of myself as good in a crisis. But for a while it fit.

It was a taxing job on the best of days, and besides my bereavement leave, there was no slow and steady ease back into the role.

Initially, I wasn't going to work when Lola was born, and instead of listening to everyone and sticking to the plan and staying home, I got my job back.

I told myself I could keep busy, and despite Jesse's insistence, we needed the money. Jesse and I argued back and forth, back and forth, finally settling on me working part-time. But in hindsight, even that was too much.

Two weeks wasn't enough time for me to process our loss. But if I still wanted my job, two weeks of bereavement leave was all I was allowed. We were now coming close to fifteen months and I still wasn't any closer to processing it.

As my grief settled in, and life without her began to take shape, I couldn't walk into work or our home without being reminded of our loss. I felt it like a gut punch, every day. Add in the high stress and pressure of the job itself and I was nothing more than walking flesh and bone.

"I don't know what could suit me right now," I say honestly. "The days all feel very different. Plus, I'm doing the outpatient rehab and therapy with Jesse. I probably couldn't commit to anything full-time right now, but I need to start helping Jesse with our finances."

Gio rests his elbows on the table in front of him and clasps his hands together. His eyes look thoughtful, but something tells me I'm not going to like whatever it is he wants to tell me.

"What is it?" I ask.

"I don't think you should go back to work just yet." I open my mouth to argue and he puts a hand up between us. "Hear me out first."

My hands find empty sugar packets on the table and I begin to nervously rip at them, waiting for him to speak.

"You seem different lately," he observes.

My face scrunches up in confusion. "But what's that got to do with me getting a job?"

"It's a good different. Like you're maybe ready to come out from that fog you've been living in for the past year. And I don't think a job should really rank high on your to-do list, or even at all, right now."

I'm grateful for the compliment, but even more so I'm grateful to him for noticing. But it feels too early. Too soon. Like I'm standing out in the open air and if the wind blows too hard, I'll topple and be right back where I started.

I still don't feel grounded or even remotely equipped to deal with Lola's death, but being back home, in Jesse's presence, and in therapy, means something has to give. It was much easier to wallow at Gio's because, for all intents and purposes, I didn't owe him anything.

We didn't have vows, we hadn't made promises, we weren't parents, and Gio and I didn't lose our baby girl.

Jesse deserves more. He deserves more than the shell of a husband I am, and I need to at least try and be more than that.

For him.

For Raine.

For me.

"But being able to contribute to our finances will make me feel useful," I explain. "I'm not really bringing anything else to the table right now."

Gio reaches across the table and stills my hands. "You know as well as I do Jesse doesn't give a shit about the money. He would rather see you making strides any day of the week."

"I know, but..." My words trail off as my leg begins bouncing anxiously underneath the table. "I don't like being home alone," I confess. "When there's nothing to distract me, Lola not being in that house with us is all I think about."

Gio's face softens, his smile sad. "Just tell Jesse that. Don't try to figure it all out at once and stunt your progress."

"I want to love being in our house," I state. "We were so happy when we bought it."

Gio doesn't offer false comforts or fill the silence with words. He watches me as I get lost in my own thoughts about all the ways I wish things could be better.

"How's the drinking?" Gio asks. He averts his gaze after asking, trying to seem as nonchalant as possible. Like whatever my answer is isn't going to be a big deal.

I have yet to admit I have a problem to myself or out loud. I'm finding it really hard to label myself as an alcoholic, because the shame that comes with being exactly like my parents is something I'm not ready to unpack.

"I haven't left the house to drink," I tell him. What I don't add is that there have been one or two days where I have managed not to drink at all. There is a vulnerable part of me that wants recognition and praise every time I make a change, but the cynic in me chooses to hold back, certain that it doesn't matter, because nothing will really change.

He nods, and I allow him to read between the lines and make his own assumptions about what that means and whether he thinks it's good or bad.

Gio's phone pings and I can tell by the look on his face as he glances down at the screen he has to get back to work.

When he looks back up at me, I raise a hand to stop the words that are about to come out of his mouth. "Do not apologize for going back to work, you are not my keeper."

He purses his lips together and shakes his head. "Okay, but what are you going to do for the rest of the day?"

I shrug. "I'm a big boy, I can figure it out."

I HAD BEEN WALKING FOR AN HOUR, MY SKIN SWEATY, MY FEET aching. I'm not one for physical exertion, especially lately, but once I realized how close I was to Jesse's work, I didn't want to stop.

It's usually a fifteen minute drive between the two

places, but since driving isn't in my plans for the foreseeable future, this seemed like a good idea at the time.

But now that I'm here, and out of breath, I realize this was probably the dumbest idea I've had today. He doesn't want to see me, not here of all places. This is his space without me, where he probably doesn't have to worry about everything else going on at home.

"Leo." I turn my head to the sound of my name to see Deacon, Jesse's boss, getting out of his car and walking toward me. He smiles, wide and genuine. "It's so good to see you." Holding out his hand, he tips his head to the garage. "I'm guessing you're here to see Jesse?"

I shake his hand. "Yeah. If that's okay? I was just in the area," I answer awkwardly.

"Of course. Of course." He leads me to the customer entrance of the garage and I follow him inside.

It's a nice sized seating area, carpeted, with a few wooden coffee tables and chairs scattered around for people as they wait to pick up their cars.

There's a desk directly opposite the door that usually has their receptionist, Demi, sitting behind it, but today it's empty.

The office phone starts ringing and Deacon groans. "Sorry, give me a second. Demi moved to Colorado and it's chaos without her."

I watch him walk behind the desk, phone still in hand, and flip through what looks to be an appointment book. About two minutes pass when he puts a hand over the receiver and glances at the door that leads to the main garage. "Go on in," he says. "Jesse will be easy to spot, just watch yourself if you can."

I offer a nervous smile as he resumes his phone call, and I push open the heavy glass door.

The smells and sounds of cars permeate the air around me, the tinkering of metal on metal echoes off the large garage walls.

My eyes dance around the area, mindful of my presence in a potentially hazardous place.

When a familiar dark brown head of hair pops out from underneath a hood, my heart starts to beat wildly with every step.

In another life, I did this all the time.

In another life, I wouldn't feel like jumping out of my skin at the prospect of surprising my husband at work.

"Leo?"

So caught up in my own head, I don't realize he's already noticed me. His eyes are wide and full of panic, and it hits me just how different spontaneity looks like after you've suffered through a trauma.

Almost like anything unexpected would forever be bad news.

I answer his unspoken question, *needing* to ease his panic. "Everything's fine. I just finished seeing Gio and thought I would come to see you too."

His shoulders visibly relax, but I don't miss the confusion that now settles in his gaze. It hurts to see, but not as much as the residual trauma he too is keeping bottled inside.

"Do you have time for a break?" I ask.

He glances past me, and I lower my head to my chest to avoid seeing whatever exchange goes on between him and the person behind me.

There's no doubt everybody here is aware of the state of Jesse's and my marriage. This is *his* safe space and these are *his* friends. I'm certain they aren't judging me, but I don't want to see whatever it is he's trying to convey to them right now.

"Yeah," he finally answers. "I've got some time."

This time I let him lead me out of the garage, to the staff break room. I watch him open the fridge and pull out a cooler bag and two bottles of water.

"I brought lunch," he says, turning to face me.

I smile, because for as long as I've known him, he's always taken his own food to work.

"Do you want some?"

"I'm good watching you eat."

He tips his head up to the ceiling. "Wade won't shut up about how good the weather is lately, it'll be nice to eat on the roof."

Following him up a steep set of stairs, my eyes fix themselves on the way the sturdy material of his pants stretches over his ass and thighs.

I don't realize I'm lost in my own thoughts and staring till I hear him say my name.

"Sorry," I say as we reach the top of the landing. "What did you say?"

He smirks knowingly, and I just shrug. "I asked you how Gio was."

"Oh, yeah, he's fine. Same as always."

He chuckles, stepping toward me. Reaching for me, he trails his fingers down the side of my face. His expression is soft and tender.

"You look beautiful like this," he says softly before pressing his lips to the corner of mine.

The moment passes quicker than I want it to and Jesse is off to find us somewhere to sit, and I'm once again admiring the man who can find the time to compliment me amongst all of the chaos I've caused him.

The rooftop is nothing more than a concrete space with the same chair and table arrangement as downstairs. There's half a shade sail that covers a quarter of the space and the rest is currently being inundated with sunlight.

Jesse sits us right where the sun meets the shade, giving us the best of both worlds. Across from one another, I watch him start to unpack his cooler bag.

His phone vibrates on the table between us and I see a text from Raine on the screen. I swallow down the emotion-filled lump in the back of my throat.

We aren't sitting in an awkward silence now, but it isn't comfortable either. It's more of a cautious silence. A delicate silence, one with so much unfinished and so much unsaid. Everything between us is still so raw and breakable, especially when it comes to Raine.

"Do you think she'll forgive me?" I ask.

I know he wants to say yes. Instinct has him wanting to reassure me that everything would be okay, no matter what. It's second nature to him, but as he folds his arms across the table, I watch the struggle to be honest play out across his features.

The man doesn't want to break me, but he's figuring out that we aren't getting anywhere unless he learns how to be cruel to be kind. So, I wait for what I know is going to hurt.

"I don't know." He shrugs. "She won't tell anyone how much damage we've done."

CHAPTER FIFTEEN

THEN

"DAD, YOUR BOYFRIEND IS HERE," Raine calls out.

She's looking out the front window, staring right at Leo. He's smiling back at her, but I can see the nervousness behind it, and I'd be lying if I said I didn't actually quite love it.

There was no bigger turn-on than a man who cared about first impressions. Especially when it comes to your daughter.

"How do you know he's my boyfriend?" I ask, walking to the front door.

She shrugs. "You said he was coming over today and this man has a box that looks like donuts. I hope he's your boyfriend."

"That's all it takes, huh?" I murmur to myself. "A box of donuts?"

I open the door, with Raine now hot on my heels.

"Welcome," I greet animatedly before leaning in and kissing him on the cheek. "Raine's so excited to meet you."

Raine's head pops out from behind me. She's dressed

in an oversized sweater that has different colored cats sewn across every inch of it and a pair of jeans. She hates wearing anything but pajamas at home, so I'm grateful she decided to dress up for the occasion. Her feet are bare and her dark brown hair is in a braid that I've finally mastered.

"Hi, are those donuts?" she asks him. "Are they plain or are they flavored? Do they have sprinkles?"

"Raine," I chastise. "Where are your manners?"

"I said hi," she counters, now standing between Leo and me. "I'm Raine. What's your name?"

He hands me the box of donuts and holds his hand out for her to shake. "I'm Leo."

"There's a Leo in my class at school," she tells him. "But his actual name is Leonardo. Is that your name too?"

"It is," he answers. "It's my grandfather's name, actually. I was named after him."

"Dad." Raine looks up at me. "Who did you name me after?"

"Umm, I can't remember. I'm pretty sure we put our favorite names into a hat and then whichever one we picked out won."

"Really?" She looks absolutely appalled.

"That's way better if you ask me," Leo says, trying to distract her from my parental faux pas. "Because nobody else has your name. Do you spell it like the word rain? R-A-I-N?"

She shakes her head. "No, it's R-A-I-N-E."

"Oh, so really your name is Rain-e?"

"No," she drolls. "It's rain with an e."

"That's what I said. Rain-e." Leo's expression is serious as he meets my gaze. "That's her name, right?"

I bite on my bottom lip to refrain from laughing. "I'll

have to check with her mom, maybe we got the spelling wrong."

She rolls her eyes, clearly exasperated by us, and grabs the box of donuts out of my hands. "I'll be in the kitchen if you need me."

"I think there's one of each," Leo calls out behind her. "Plain, sprinkles and chocolate."

I catch her trying to balance the box and lift the lid at the same time as she walks to the kitchen, counting and murmuring to herself.

"Do you think she hates me?" Leo asks. "I think the donuts might help smooth things over."

"She's ten going on twenty," I tell him. "She can hold her own, don't you worry." I tug him to me, resting my hands on his waist. "Right now she only cares about those donuts and is probably scheming on how to eat one before dinner without me noticing. Her dad and his boyfriend are no longer a priority."

He raises his arms and wraps them around my neck, his cheeks flushed, his smile wide. "I can't believe I'm her dad's boyfriend."

"Only because you haven't yet agreed to be my husband."

His smile remains. "You know I'm waiting for you to ask one thousand times before I say yes."

"You say it like I have an issue with asking you one thousand times."

"Really? The rejection doesn't sting?" he asks.

"You haven't rejected me once," I say confidently. He bites the inside of his cheek as I add, "All I've been hearing is 'not now.'"

"Sometimes I just want to rip that cocky look right off your face," he says.

"And sometimes you want to kiss it." I press my mouth to his quickly. "Same. Same."

"Dad," Raine calls out, interrupting us. "It's almost time to watch *So You Think You Can Dance*. Can we eat dinner soon?"

He drops a quick kiss on my lips and unwraps his arms from around my neck. I take his hand in mine, leading him to the kitchen. We catch Raine surreptitiously wiping a smear of chocolate off the corner of her mouth.

Leo turns to look at me quickly, his eyes full of humor as he tilts his head to Raine. We both do our best not to laugh.

"What's for dinner?" Leo asks Raine.

"It's one of my favorites," she replies, completely oblivious to us catching her in the act. "Dad made cheeseburgers with homemade fries. And I helped with peeling the potatoes."

"Do you help your dad cook all the time?"

"Only when it's my favorite foods," she retorts.

"Sounds like you've got it all figured out." He turns his attention to me. "Need me to set the table?"

"Raine, do you want to show Leo how to set the table while I finish off the burgers?"

I only need to fry the patties, add the cheese, and toast the buns; I can do it with my eyes closed. While I move around the kitchen easily, I can't help but watch the back-and-forth between Leo and Raine.

It's easy, almost effortless.

He would try to argue with me and say it isn't possible, but I've known Leo would be an important part of my life from the moment I laid eyes on him. There was no question of whether or not I would introduce him to Zara and Raine, just a matter of when.

Now, here they are, chatting like old friends as Raine

shows him how to set the table. There's no huge production, no fanfare. It's just like it's always been, like *he's* always been.

"Raine," I call out.

"Yeah."

"Ask Leo if he'll marry me."

She looks at me like I've grown two heads but turns to him anyway. "Will you marry my dad?"

"I told him he has to ask me a thousand times before I say yes."

This has piqued her interest. "And how many times has he asked you?"

He bends down till his mouth is at her ear and uses his hand to shield his lips so I can't read them. His voice is just above a whisper but even then, I can't hear what he says to her. Her brown eyes dart to mine and she smiles at me conspiratorially before adding, "You need to keep asking, because you're nowhere near one thousand."

"Are you going to tell me how many more times I have to ask?"

"I can't, Dad," she says seriously. "That would be cheating."

"Cheating," I exclaim and glance at Leo. "No loyalty to her dad."

Leo laughs at my statement and shrugs, enjoying the camaraderie they have so easily developed.

They're going to be trouble together, and I've never been more excited.

"Okay, you two. Bring the plates up here and put these burgers together," I announce. "I'm going to start deep frying the fries."

As I pour the oil into the deep fryer and turn it on to heat up, I hear Raine explain to Leo that I've already cut up some lettuce and tomatoes and plated some pickles to be used as garnish on the burgers. And that we have four different cheeses for him to choose from but she will only be eating the shitty processed cheese that her dad hates.

"Hey," I reprimand. "Only I get to call it shitty."

She shrugs, completely unbothered by me, before returning her attention to Leo. "Which cheese will you eat?"

Smirking, I turn to look at him, and he's deep in thought, eyes darting between the processed, cheddar, swiss, and pepper-jack. Straightening his spine, he folds his arms across his chest, rearranging them a few times for emphasis, before tapping his chin with his finger as if he's concentrating. "I think you're right. Shitty cheese is the winner."

She jumps up in the air in excitement and then raises her hand for him to high five. "Guess you're on your own, Dad."

"I guess I am," I murmur under my breath, too busy smiling to even care.

Leo appears holding up two plates and I place burger buns and beef patties with cheese on either one.

"Here, Rain-e," he calls out. "Put your burger together so I can put one together for your dad."

"Who's Rain-e?" she asks, mortified, as she takes her plate off of him. "That's not my name."

"But that's how you said you spell it, isn't it?"

She scrunches up her face in disapproval, clearly trying to come up with a logical reason as to why it's spelled differently than the way it's said. Struggling to make sense of it all, she snatches her plate off of him and huffs. "Fine, you can call me Rain-e. But nobody else, okay?"

I hear her warning loud and clear.

It's another ten minutes until we're sitting down at the table together, burgers constructed, hot homemade fries on the side. There's nothing but contentment between the three of us as we all dig into our food. Raine is silent, enjoying her cheeseburger, and Leo and I are exchanging stupid, goofy, love-struck smiles.

"Oh no, we forgot our drinks." Raine hops up quickly and walks to the fridge, awkwardly grabbing three cans of soda and slamming the door with her foot. She puts a can in front of each of us before sitting down.

"You've got to be kidding me," Leo says, disgust written all over his face. "She likes Dr. Pepper too?"

FULL AND SATED, LEO AND I SIT, STRETCHED OUT ON THE COUCH, Raine comfortably lying on her stomach on the floor.

"Do you dance?" Leo asks her during a commercial break.

"No," Raine replies without looking at him. I notice the slightest slump in her shoulders as she continues to look at the television but answers his question, her voice soft and unsure. "I'm not very good, and I don't want to dance in front of people."

It's the first time I've heard a word of any of this. I wonder how long she's been bottling it up and why she's only bringing it up now.

I go to open my mouth and Leo places a hand on my thigh, stopping me.

"I bet you're a better dancer than me," he says to her.

She presses pause on the television remote and shifts her body enough to face us but not completely get herself up off the floor, her expression disbelieving.

"He really is a terrible dancer," I tell her. "Probably the worst I've ever seen."

Leo raises an eyebrow at me. "The worst you've ever seen? Really?"

My shoulders rise and fall. "If the shoe fits."

"Dad, that's so rude," Raine chastises. "You can't just tell someone they're a terrible dancer."

"Even if it's the truth?"

"Even if it's the truth," she says firmly.

"But you haven't even seen him dance yet," I counter. "I bet I can get you to change your mind." I nudge Leo on the shoulder. "Put a song on and dance. Show her."

If he's embarrassed or annoyed at being put on the spot, I can't tell. Instead, he pulls his cell out of his pocket and throws it to Raine. "Pick a song."

She seems to navigate his phone with ease, and I marvel at how kids her age don't need an introduction to technology. Her fingers tap away until a song I've never heard fills the living room.

"I love this song," Leo exclaims. "Will you dance with me?"

He bobs over to Raine and holds his hand out for her to take. Hesitantly, she takes his offer and he pulls her up till they're both standing, Leo moving to the beat while Raine stands there nervously.

He picks up the pace, his arms and legs now just flailing, and I catch Raine's widened eyes. If I wasn't so enamored by him the night we met, I'm certain I would've stared at him the exact same way.

When her gaze shifts to me, I mouth *I told you so,* and the sweetest giggle leaves her mouth.

"Come on," Leo coaxes. "Show me what you got."

Hand in hand, they move all around the living room in

the most coordinated uncoordinated dance I have ever seen. Raine's eyes are bright, her smile pure undiluted joy. It was the same exact look that made me notice Leo that night; a smile that beamed from the inside out.

The song ends and another one starts as they continue to purposefully dance worse than the other. They laugh and sing and my heart grows to an unmanageable size.

I rub a fist over my chest. There's no denying I'm in love with him. Hard and fast. I'm so happy it hurts, but the possibility of losing what I'm feeling in this moment could easily bring me to my knees.

Our eyes meet over Raine's head and I lose the ability to keep those three words to myself.

"*I love you,*" I mouth.

I watch the words land as he bends and whispers something into Raine's ear. Nodding, she runs up to me, grabbing my hand and pulling me up off the couch.

"Dance with us, Dad," she exclaims over the music.

I let her lead me to Leo, and when I reach him, he takes my free hand and raises it to his chest, right atop his heart.

He leans into me, mouth right by my ear. "Feel it," he says, placing his hand over mine. His heart beats wildly against my palm. "It only does that for you."

CHAPTER SIXTEEN

THEN

"WHAT DO you mean you got her dance lessons?" Jesse exclaims.

"I got *us* dance lessons," I correct. "They're for me and Raine."

Jesse and I are sitting beside one another at one of our favorite Greek restaurants, waiting for the server to bring out our usual order. The table is round, and no matter how many times we start the night sitting opposite one another, we always end up side by side, waiting for our food to arrive, our bodies facing each other, knees knocking, hands roaming.

"You got dance lessons for Raine?" he asks incredulously.

For a split second I can't tell if he's impressed or upset, and I internally panic that maybe I've overstepped. I probably should've asked for Jesse's permission before assuming I could organize just anything for his daughter.

"Fuck. I should've asked you first," I say. "Or even Zara. Shit. I honestly didn't think you would have a problem with it."

"No," he interjects quickly, placing a hand over my thigh and squeezing. "That is absolutely not it. Sorry for freaking you out. I'm just surprised."

"Good surprised or bad surprised?"

He smiles, and the knot of anxiety in my stomach loosens. "Good. Of course it's good. You just didn't have to do that."

I straighten my spine, my voice serious. "I want to do things for her. I know you don't expect it, but she is part of..." I gesture between us. "Whatever this is for me."

His hold on my thigh loosens as he starts to move his hand higher. "And what is this for you?"

Smirking, I place my hand over his, stilling him. "Don't you start distracting me. We were talking about Raine and dancing lessons."

"Okay. Okay. You're right." He rolls his shoulders and puts his hands up in surrender. "Tell me about the dancing."

"Okay." I clap my hands together excitedly. "It took me a while to find something that wasn't a class with twenty or thirty other kids," I explain. "And a teacher willing to spend an hour teaching only one child, but persistence paid off and a great opportunity came through."

His brows furrow in concentration. "You got her one-on-one lessons?"

"Of course I did. You heard how nervous she was about dancing in front of other people."

He catches me completely off guard when he curls his hand around my nape and buries his head in the crook of my neck.

"Marry me," he murmurs against my pulse.

I bite back the moan that wants to slip out of my mouth and rest a hand on his thigh. We are never going to get through this conversation, let alone dinner at this rate. "Jesse," I groan.

"Don't 'Jesse' me, when you're here telling me all the effort you're going through to get my daughter her own private dance lessons," he says into my ear. "You expect me to keep my hands off you when all they want to do is thank you?"

"I promise," I breathe out. "You can thank me later. More than once."

"Fine. Fine. Fine," he says loudly. He rises up off the chair, and I watch him move it across the table and take a seat. "Tell me the rest of it."

I couldn't stop the smile from spreading across my face. I will never get over just how much he loves being close to me. Kissing me. Seducing me. Loving me. He has a way to touch me for every occasion.

"So, I came across this dance studio," I continue. "And when I explained the situation, the owner mentioned that her teenage daughter is in the process of getting herself accredited as a dance teacher and if I was okay with it, she could practice teaching Raine and me."

"You really want to dance with her?" he asks me.

"It's been months of us binging reruns of *So You Think You Can Dance* and us dancing together in the living room. I think she'll love it," I say truthfully. "And maybe me being there, showing her how ridiculous I am, will help take off the pressure she's putting on herself to be perfect."

Over the time I've spent with Raine, it was evident that she is an overachiever. She hates failure, and the expectation she puts on herself not to fail is too high for someone her age. I'd heard both Zara and Jesse tell her repeatedly that her best efforts would always be enough.

It's obvious she has yet to believe them.

"What's the worst thing that can happen?" I ask him. "We spend one afternoon a week dancing? I don't see a problem with it."

"And how much is it?"

I know he didn't mean anything by the question, because he was just a father taking care of his daughter with no expectations that I needed to do the same, but I didn't want it to be that way.

I want him to know that anything I do for Raine is because I want to, and that includes paying for her dance lessons.

"You're not paying, so you don't need to know how much it is."

He shakes his head. "No, you can't," he argues. "That's too much and she's my—"

It didn't matter that while the teacher was pretty much free, the studio time was highway robbery. If I have to sell my whole world to make sure I can afford her dance lessons, that's what I'll do. There is no way I'll let him pay for something I want to give to her.

"I know." I cut him off from finishing. "She's your daughter."

Hating the space between us, it's my turn to rise up from my seat and move my chair closer to him. Sitting beside him, I lean in and plant a soft kiss on his cheek. "It's because she's yours that I want to do this. Just let me, okay?"

GIDDY WAS AN UNDERSTATEMENT.

Zara and Jesse and I had decided that we would leave the dance lessons as a surprise, but since this is the first time all three adults and Raine have been in a car together, I'm certain she knows something is going on.

"Where are we going?" she asks for the tenth time.

"To the zoo," Jesse responds at the same time Zara says "Chihuly Garden and Glass."

Sitting in the front beside Jesse, who's driving, I shift my body to make it easier to look back at her. "Where do you think we're going?"

She glances down at the shorts and t-shirt she's been instructed to wear and then back at me, who is also dressed in something similar.

"Why is it only me and Leo who are dressed the same?" she asks.

"I just came back from the gym," I lie.

She eyes me skeptically but remains silent as she looks out the window, completely fed up with the three of us.

It only takes another five minutes before Jesse pulls into the studio parking lot and a huge sign at the top of the building reads 'Dance It Out.'

Zara and I both keep our eyes focused on Raine, not wanting to miss the moment of realization. I'd be lying if I said I wasn't nervous about her reaction. I don't want her worry about dancing in front of other people to overshadow any potential excitement.

Her eyes dart around the car, looking at each of us. "What are we doing here?" she asks, her voice full of nerves.

Zara throws an arm around her. "You're going to take dance lessons."

Raine wrings her hands together, and I can see her start to pick at her cuticles. I don't think I'll even be able to get her inside if I don't tell her the rest and ease her worry.

"It'll just be me and you," I tell her. "That's why we're dressed the same."

She looks between our outfits and then back at me. "We're going to dance lessons?"

I nod. "Every Thursday afternoon."

"Only you and me?" she presses, and I know she isn't asking because she's curious to see if her parents are joining us.

"Yes. You and me and the instructor," I inform her. "Nobody else will be there, except maybe Mom and Dad if they want to watch."

I see the weight immediately lift off of her as I paint the complete picture. "You'll get to meet the teacher and decide what form of dance you want to learn."

At this stage, Jesse has parked the car and he, too, has turned to look at her. All our focus is on the beating heart of this unconventional family.

Because that is what this is. It's a family. I didn't need extravagant words or displays of affection to know that I had been accepted by all of them.

They are mine, just as much as I'm theirs.

CHAPTER SEVENTEEN

NOW

THE PASSENGER DOOR FLIES OPEN.

"Sorry if I kept you waiting," Leo huffs out as he climbs into the car. "So many people wanted to share stuff today and the timing went all over the place."

"It's okay," I respond. "It happens."

"I know, but I don't want to be late to Dr. Sosa."

His words and actions lately were a far cry from the man who refused to start therapy with me in the first place. And I'm still coming to terms with the change.

I'm not sure why I'm distancing myself, because every part of me, for so long, has been desperate to put us all back together, and now I feel like I'm the only thing stopping it.

"How was your day?" Leo asks.

"Good," I answer. "And yours?"

Today, Leo had both outpatient rehab and our appointment with Dr. Sosa after. I offered to cancel the latter when I found out about his schedule clash, but Leo insisted he could handle both on the same day.

"It was fine," he answers casually. "I'll be glad to see the back of these sessions."

I glance at him quickly before focusing my attention on the road and veering the car away from the building and back into traffic.

"You don't find them useful?"

"I do. But I'm hoping to try more one-on-one stuff after it ends," he explains. "Something a little more tailored to me and what I'm dealing with."

Again, I feel so off balance by his decision to move forward and want the changes.

"And what is it you're dealing with?" The question bites and we both hear it.

"Jesse."

I've always loved the way Leo says my name—with a lifetime of love and reverence—and now it is nothing more than a longing I feel down to my bones.

"I'm sorry," I say, my voice a little softer. "I'm just struggling."

It isn't a lie and it isn't the truth, but it's all I can give.

The rest of the drive is silent, and when we arrive at Dr. Sosa's, Leo can't get out of the car quick enough. As I drag my feet behind him, I have to wonder if this is how Leo has felt every time we've been here. So overwhelmed and help-less and undeniably broken.

"Leo. Jesse. It's good to see you both. Come in."

Dr. Sosa is already waiting for us, and I'm grateful there isn't the usual delay in the waiting room.

Seated with my arms resting on my thighs and my head hanging low, I'm surprised when I hear Leo's voice before Dr. Sosa's.

"I think I might've pushed Jesse too far," he says.

My head snaps up to catch him looking at me.

"What makes you say that?" Dr. Sosa asks.

He shrugs. "Maybe I just took too long."

"Too long for what?" she presses.

He shrugs again. "I want to be better. Well, I'm trying to anyway."

"That's not fair," I blurt out. "You don't get to say you're trying like it fixes everything, like the damage hasn't already been done."

"I didn't say anything was fixed," he argues. "I said maybe I've taken too long, like maybe now that I can see some light, you're over it."

I want to punch a wall or maybe throw a chair across the room. I want to be anywhere but within these four walls.

Closing my eyes, I tilt my head up to the ceiling. I breathe and count.

I count to ten. Inhale.

I count to twenty. Exhale

"I'm here," I say, not to either of them specifically. "I'm here and I'm not over it."

When I find the strength to open my eyes, I look straight at Dr. Sosa. "If I'm not trying to keep him in the present, if I'm not trying to limit his self-destruction, I don't know who I am.

"I went from husband to caretaker in a matter of days," I explain. "I don't even think I was able to make a pit stop at grieving father. It has been me spending months and months and months getting him to this exact point."

Finally, I shift my gaze to his. "Don't tell me I'm over it, because I'm not fucking over it. I'm just fucking tired."

The silence builds as we stare at each other, Leo fighting off tears while I sit here riddled with tension.

"Jesse," Dr. Sosa finally says. "I'm going to go ahead and

say you've been the one to make sure everyone in your family is okay after Lola's death."

"He has," Leo answers. "He's always been the glue. He holds us all together."

I wanted to be that man; I had lived to be that man. But for the first time in my entire life, I have never hated anything more than I hate being the glue right now.

"And, Jesse, what do you do to hold yourself together?"

"Nothing." The answer leaves my mouth much quicker than I intend it to. I drop my chin to my chest, keeping my eyes fixed on the floor, my silence answering her question.

"Do you think you could tell Leo the things you need from him right now?"

Being in this room has always been so confronting. The layout, the proximity, the feeling of being completely exposed. It almost feels like a boxing ring, each person on either side, each truth, each flaw, each lie a punch straight to the chest.

And there was Dr. Sosa, coaxing you to get up, pushing you to try one more time.

I don't have anything else left in me; one more hit and I'm going to bleed out here on her floor.

"He isn't going to know what you need unless you tell him."

"Just like that." The sarcasm is dripping from my voice as I look directly at Leo. "What do you need me to tell you? Because my daughter died too. My daughter lost a sister too. My best friend carried a baby that didn't survive too."

The words just hang, and for the first time, I don't regret them. If anything, I feel like I've taken my very first breath in over twelve months.

I didn't say that to hurt him. I didn't say it to punish

him. It's just a reminder that I was there. I went through it too. I am sad and lonely and lost too.

"Leo, do you want to say anything to that?" Dr. Sosa asks him.

He doesn't avert his eyes, nor do they fill with tears. The only indication he's even the slightest bit affected by my outburst is the movement of his throat and jaw.

"I didn't think our grief was the same," he says, and it completely throws me for a loop. "I told myself you already have a family, so it probably didn't hurt you as much."

And there it is, the hit I needed to bleed out.

"How can you say that?" My voice is nothing but shards of glass. "How can you even think that?"

"I know it's not true," he says, trying to appease me. He leans forward in his seat, almost like he wants to reach for me. "Subconsciously I think I always knew that. I just wanted to justify my pain. I wanted to justify how long it was taking me to get my shit together. I only felt like I was weighing you down."

"Do you still feel like that?" I ask, the words sounding every bit as dejected as I feel. "All of it. Do you still feel like that?"

"Every day I feel like I'm weighing you down," he confesses. "But the assumptions about your pain and grief—"

"No." I cut him off. "That I have a family that doesn't include you?" I don't even wait for an answer before my uncensored thoughts fly out of my mouth. "What have I ever done that has made you feel or think like that?"

"Jesse," Dr. Sosa interrupts. "For some people there is no rational thinking when it comes to their grief and processing it. A lot of the time, trauma can skew our perceptions and the way we see the world around us."

I know she's right. When Leo found out he was sterile, he and I had conversations that were very reminiscent of this, but I thought he had moved past it. I thought *we* had moved past it.

Either way, I still just want her to shut up. I want her to fuck off with her logic and her facts and just let me and Leo be. I want a conversation with my husband where we are allowed to tear each other to shreds and then spend the rest of the night apologizing to one another.

I'm so sick of all of it.

I shoot straight up out of my chair and look between both of them. "I can't do any more of this today," I tell them. "I'm sorry, but I just don't have it in me right now to think coherent, reasonable thoughts."

I don't wait for permission or approval before storming out of her office. I don't even give either of them the chance to stop me. When I reach the car, I open the driver's door only to slam it again.

I do it again.

And again.

And again.

"You're going to break the door," Leo says, his voice steady.

"Maybe I want to break it," I retort petulantly.

"Do you want me to find my own way home?"

Resigned, I shake my head. "Don't be stupid."

Wordlessly, I fold myself into the car and wait for Leo to climb in. Before I can start the car, he places his hand on my forearm. "Can we go visit Lola?"

My hands are shoved deep in my pockets as I stand at the end of Lola's grave. It's such a small space for someone who holds such a large place in our lives. The air's cold on my skin as the afternoon sun hides behind clouds. I don't know what Leo wants to do here, but I can't deny the sense of calmness that's washed over me.

Surprising me, Leo wraps his arms around my middle. He rests his head in the middle of my back, just below my neck, and I can't help but cover his arms with mine.

It's so simple, but it's also been so long since someone has held me instead of the other way around.

"I'm sorry," he says. "I'm sorry I've been so selfish in my grief. And I—"

"Leo," I breathe out.

"No," he says firmly. Dropping his arms, he places a hand on my hip and guides me to turn around and face him. Stepping closer, he absorbs all the distance between us before placing a hand on either side of my face. "No," he repeats, his eyes boring into mine. "You have to stop excusing my behavior. Especially at the expense of your own feelings. I'm sorry," he says again, softer, his touch now gentle. "I'm sorry I made you bypass being a grieving father."

I shake my head as my chest heaves and the tears I've held on to for too damn long stream down my face.

No longer the glue, I find myself being held together by arms and legs and low whispers. My head is buried in the curve of his neck as we both fall to the cold grass, crying.

"I'm sorry I wasn't by your side like the husband I vowed to be," he says. "Like the husband you've been to me." My shoulders shake as he continues. "I'm so sorry for leaving you to grieve alone."

The seconds turn into minutes as his hold on me tightens, apology after apology leaving his mouth. Just as I manage to catch my breath, he presses his lips to my temple and whispers, "You lost your daughter too. And I am so, so sorry for your loss."

CHAPTER EIGHTEEN

then

LEO

TODAY IS THE DAY.

Dragging a bunch of keys out of my pocket, I flip through them all, searching for the one I need. I've had Jesse's house key in my possession for almost a year now, him secretly hoping I would move in, or better yet, agree to marry him.

Sliding the key into the lock, I turn it and push the front door open. As expected, both Zara and Raine are sitting on the couch waiting for me.

"Thank God, you're finally here." Raine bounces off the couch and runs to me. She's a year off becoming a teenager but it seems like she never gets too old to hug me, and I love that.

"Sorry," I say, "I got held up picking up what I needed from my place and from the store."

I glance over Raine's head and catch Zara smiling at the two of us.

"How are you feeling?" she asks.

"Nervous. You?"

"Not nervous," she answers. "But I'm not the one proposing tonight either."

I don't even get a chance to respond when Raine interjects. "I can't believe you actually waited for Dad to ask you one thousand times before saying yes."

Raine's statement isn't exactly the truth, but it's probably the only way to explain the method to my madness. In actual fact, I had said yes to myself every single time. From the first proposal to the thousandth, I have never wavered in wanting to marry Jesse Hunt.

At some point I started to wait for a "real" proposal, but it wasn't until one day I overheard him casually talking to Zara that I realized he didn't think I was really interested in marriage, and if that was the case he would be with me in whatever way that looked like.

It both broke my heart and made me fall even harder for him. On one hand, had I really made him think that marriage wasn't an option? And on the other, there was nothing this man wouldn't do for me, and that included sacrificing his own wants and needs.

It was a blessing and a curse.

I *need* him to know that I could and I would make as many of his dreams come true as he did mine. And that included becoming his husband.

"If someone really wants to marry you," I tell Raine as I throw her over my shoulder, grab the bags I came in with, and walk to the kitchen. "Make sure they ask you to marry them one thousand times before you say yes, okay?"

"Put me down," she squeals. "I'm twelve now."

"I don't care if you're a hundred," I exclaim.

I sit her down on the kitchen counter and she scrunches up her face at me. "What if I don't want to get married?"

I rub the small crease between her brows. "Then you don't get married. We don't do things we don't want to do."

She smirks. "So, no chores, no homework, no early bedtime?"

I bop her on the nose. "You wish. Now, are you going to help me or not?"

Zara appears in the kitchen after us, her cell phone in hand. "Jesse just texted. I told him he didn't need to pick up Raine and that will buy us some more time."

"Perfect," I say as I unpack the ingredients I bought for dinner.

"Are you sure you're going to be okay with this risotto?" Zara asks me. "You leave it in the slow cooker for two hours. Don't touch it, don't open it, don't smell it till the two hours are up."

I salute her. "Yes, ma'am."

"Thank you for including us," Zara says as she starts organizing everything she needs to fry up.

"What are you even talking about?" I whirl around to face her. "In what world would I not include you?"

"I'm just saying—"

"Just stop *saying*. Please. I don't want to do this without your help," I tell her. My eyes then dart between the two of them. "You and Raine are my favorite package deal." I waggle my eyebrows suggestively. "And there will be parts that you're not here for."

Smiling, she raises her palm to my cheek, and I lean into her touch. "I don't want to hear about the parts I'm not here for, but I am so glad he found you."

Endless amounts of gratitude and love swim in my veins. "In case I haven't ever said it or don't say it enough, thank you for accepting me into your family."

Maneuvering between the two of them, I kiss them

both on the forehead. "Now, let's get this show on the road."

I ASSIGN EVERY ONE OF US A JOB AS OPERATION PROPOSING TO Jesse is in full swing. I have no plans for it to be big or elaborate, because we don't work in big sweeping gestures.

Since the very beginning, it's been the small, intimate things that hold the most sincerity and truth between us. And I want this to be exactly that.

Zara agrees to cook Jesse's favorite meal for me, because even after two years together, I have not yet learned how to master a mushroom risotto. She's making me the "dummies" version where the slow cooker does all the work, because she isn't going to be here the whole time to check on it. And Raine and I have been delegated to setting the table for two.

"Leo," Raine says, and I can hear the shake in her voice instantly.

I put the handful of cutlery on the table and stand to my full height, giving her all my attention. "What's up, Rain-e girl?"

"Can I ask you something?"

"Always."

"I asked Mom, but she said to ask you." At the mention of Zara, my gaze shifts to the kitchen and I catch her knowing smile. "If you marry Dad, are you my dad too?" My breath catches in my throat, and I'm grateful she isn't even waiting for me to answer before she continues talking. "Because you know Priscilla from school, her mom married a man and he's her stepdad now, and she said she asked him if she could call him

Dad, and Mom said the same thing, so I wanted to ask you."

It was a lot of words for such a petite girl.

A lot of words that meant so many things.

Feeling a little lightheaded, I take a seat at the table. "You want to call me Dad?" I ask, just for clarification.

"Well, you're kind of like my dad already," she says matter-of-factly. "You do all the things both Mom and Dad do with me."

"I do?"

She rolls her eyes. "You help me with my homework, take me to school, give me money if I need it. And we dance together And you—"

I cut her off. "Come here, Rain-e girl."

She takes the few steps toward me, her expression apprehensive. I reach for her hands and hold them in mine. "It would be the greatest privilege of my life to be your dad."

"I told you," Zara shouts from the kitchen.

And Raine does nothing but smile at me. From ear to ear, her crooked smile on full display. She's undoubtedly one of the best things to ever happen to me.

"But wait!" She jumps on the spot impatiently. "I can't call you Dad because that's for Dad."

"Okay."

I wait to see where her thoughts will take this conversation.

"So it needs to be different but the same."

"Not a hard request at all," I murmur through a smile. "Do you have any ideas?"

I don't care if she continues to call me Leo for the rest of our lives, but because she wants to give me the title, I want it even more.

I give her hands a reassuring squeeze. "How does this sound? When I was younger, my grandfather was my favorite person. And the most important to me. He took care of me and loved me and made sure I always had food to eat and a warm bed to sleep in," I share. "All the things that a dad does. And I called him Papa."

"I can call you Papa." The words rush out. "And Pa for short?"

"Absolutely."

"I can't wait to tell Dad," she says excitedly. "How long till he gets here?"

I check my watch. "We have one hour."

"Come on. Come on. Let's finish setting everything up," she exclaims.

She's a ball of energy, but before she rushes off, I hold on to her hand, stopping her from moving. "I love you, Rain-e girl."

"Love you too, Papa."

MY EMOTIONS ARE AT AN ALL-TIME HIGH AS I HEAR JESSE WALK through the front door. Raine and I also set up a little trail of clues for him around the house that I knew he would notice the second he walked through the door. Eventually they will lead him to me.

"Leo," he calls out.

"In here."

I'm anxiously standing in the middle of his bedroom with an array of personalized cards strewn out all over his bed. The idea is super cheesy, but short of waiting for him to propose to me one more time, when I'll actually say yes, this feels right.

"What's this?" he asks, holding up a rectangular card. I know it has the words "Marry Me" on the front and "Yes" on the back. Each card is date stamped, and from the look on his face, he's just about to ask me why. "What do these dates mean?"

Stepping closer to him, I pluck the card out of his hand and point to the date under the words "Marry Me."

"This is the date of the first time you asked me to marry you." I turn the card. "And this is the date of when I've said yes."

He narrows his eyes at the numbers as I watch his face eventually even out in recognition. "That's today's date." He cradles my face. "Does this mean what I think it means?"

I place my hands over his. "I don't know, tell me what you think it means."

He glances around the room, noticing the rest of the cards. "How many of these did you make?"

"How many do you think?"

I can see his brain ticking, thinking of all the times he's asked me to marry him. "You kept track of every proposal?" he asks, awed.

Grabbing his hips, I tug him to me. He's all greased up from work, stains on his hands and clothes, looking every bit the man of my dreams.

His thumbs dance across my cheeks as his warm chocolate eyes trace the lines on my face.

"I've always wanted to say yes," I tell him, my voice cracking as I spill my secrets. "But you know I get in my own head sometimes, make up these ridiculous rules and set these unrealistic expectations."

His lips stretch, his smile full of empathy and understanding.

"I really thought I had it all figured out when I met you," I say. "It would be one night, maybe a few repeats, and that would be it."

Jesse's smile turns into an indecent smirk. "It's been a pleasure proving you wrong."

"Don't look at me like that," I warn, the humor in my voice unmissable. "That look is for later. Right now I'm trying to tell you how much I love you."

Jesse's hands find the buttons of my shirt and his fingers begin to undo them one by one. "I don't need the words, baby. I just want your body to do the talking."

He pushes the shirt off my body and watches it fall to the floor. Grabbing hold of my hips, he turns me around and presses his mouth to the very end of my left shoulder. Soft open-mouthed kisses trail the span of my back before Jesse takes my hand and guides me to the bathroom.

We're both facing the mirror, every single detail between us on display.

His arm circles my waist, fingers finding the button on my jeans, deftly undoing it. Roughly, he pushes my pants and underwear down to the middle of my thighs, my thick cock bobbing in the air, desperate for Jesse to touch me.

He pinches the sensitive head and I hiss. "Fuck. Jesse."

I feel naked and exposed, and not just because half my clothes are missing. I watch Jesse through the mirror as he turns the shower on and then undresses himself, and my dick twitches.

It's a perfect view. My favorite view.

Completely naked, he hops in the shower and leaves the door open. I know an invitation when I see one. As soon as I step inside, Jesse is on me. He pushes me up against the cold tile, his chest pressing against my back.

"I want to hear it," he says, his warm breath on my

neck, his hand gripping my cock. "I want to hear you say the word."

I open my mouth to tell him, but he squeezes my length. "You got to wait till I ask you, baby."

I don't know how we went from me about to declare my love for this man, to him pretty much Uno reversing me and proposing to *me* during sex, but I don't care.

The details aren't important because I'm going to marry this man no matter which one of us asks, and that's the only thing that matters.

His hand finally moves up and down my cock, and my head falls back against his shoulder.

"You know the best part about being married?" he asks. "That this"—he drops his hand to my balls, rolling and squeezing them before tugging my cock again—"is all mine."

I moan obscenely loud and it echoes off the shower walls.

"You gonna marry me, baby?" he says, the words making my heart frantic and my cock throb.

"Yes," I pant. "Yes, I'll marry you."

I'm putty in his hands as he spins me around and drops to his knees, taking my cock in his mouth. My hand glides through his hair, pulling at the strands as he bobs up and down my length. My body shudders as his tongue circles the tip and glides through the slit.

"Jesus, Jesse, if you don't slow down, I'm going to come down your fucking throat."

I feel him reluctantly slide off and rise to his feet. He grips my chin, and his lips collide with mine, the taste of me on his tongue as he licks inside my mouth.

"You gonna marry me, baby?" It's always the same

words, and yet for two years they hit differently every. Fucking. Time.

I reach for his dick and line it up against mine, stretching my hand across them both. "You gonna suck my cock like that if I do?"

He groans as I jerk us both, his eyes feral. "I will fucking worship you."

"Then ask me again," I say.

"Marry me?"

"Yes," I breathe out. "Yes. Yes. Yes."

"I need inside you." He kisses me again, wet and hungry. "I need inside you right fucking now."

Grabbing his hand, I switch off the shower and lead us straight back to his bed. We are dripping water everywhere but neither one of us has it in us to care.

Positioning myself in the middle of the bed, I shamelessly bend my body, legs in the air, ass on full display. Jesse finds the bottle of lube in his bedside drawer and pours it generously around my hole before coating two fingers and the length of his cock.

Jesse climbs up onto the bed, sitting on his haunches right between my spread legs. His hand and fingers greedy for my hole. There's no finesse in the way he stretches me, his fingers impatient and desperate.

Entranced by the sight, his eyes are fixed on the way his fingers fuck me.

"I want to come home every day to you," he says, his voice like gravel, "waiting for me just like this."

"Only if you marry me," I pant.

Maneuvering himself onto all fours, Jesse lines the head of his cock with my center and slowly pushes into me. He's looking down at me as my body stretches around him, the perfect blend of love and lust glistening in his eyes.

Our foreheads press together and our breaths mingle. The room fills with nothing more than our ragged breathing as Jesse picks up the pace. His cock is so deliciously deep, expertly brushing my prostate. I'm torn between wanting to chase my release and wanting to stay in this very moment with him forever.

I loop my arms around his neck and pull him to me as he thrusts harder and faster. Determined to brand me from the inside out.

"Ask me again," he says, his voice hoarse, his control hanging by a thread.

"Marry me," I repeat.

"And again," he demands, this time grabbing my dick, intent on pushing me over the edge.

I can barely manage a coherent thought as his whole body works in perfect synchronicity to bring me to my knees.

"Jesse," I cry out. "I'm going to come."

He rolls his hips into me one last time before my orgasm ripples through me. My body shudders from head to toe, Jesse's own release following shortly after.

Limp and languid, I lie there completely boneless as Jesse collapses on top of me. I welcome the pressure as I run my fingers up and down his spine.

He is beautiful and completely sated. And all mine.

"Jesse."

He raises his head, meeting my gaze.

"Marry me."

CHAPTER NINETEEN

NOW

"HEY." I shove my hands in my pockets as Zara opens her front door. "Is she home?"

She nods, widening it enough for me to cross the threshold. "She's in her bedroom."

I lean in to kiss her on the cheek. "How are you?"

"I'm good," she says. "Big day at work, but I'm just heading to forget all about it and jump into the bath with a book."

"Did you tell her I was coming?"

She shakes her head. "You told me not to."

"I know, but what if she doesn't want to see me?"

"Maybe she won't," she says truthfully. "But you won't know if you don't try."

So much has happened. To all of us. And I'm slowly coming to terms with the fact that there is no right or wrong, or tried and true, way to deal with grief.

Every stage looked different for every person.

But what I do know? Despite the way grief manifested for each of us, as Raine's father, I had dropped the ball.

And I am her father. No matter what ugly insecurity

reared its head at the most inopportune times, I am her father and I'd failed her.

Spectacularly.

I'm standing here staring at her bedroom door, straightening my clothes, as if the way I look is going to fix any of the damage I've done, when Zara's hand reaches over my shoulder and her knuckles rap against the wood.

"You can thank me later," she whispers before walking to her own bedroom.

"Come in," a soft voice calls out.

I rub my clammy hands together before turning the handle and pushing the door open to find her lying on her stomach across her double-sized bed, feet in the air, hands flying over the keyboard of her laptop.

She doesn't look up, and I'm certain it's because she's only expecting the interruption to be Zara.

I clear my throat. "Can I come in?"

Her head whips up at the sound of my voice, her expression completely unreadable. I wait for a sign or any indication that she doesn't want me here, even some words to leave her mouth and tell me to get out, but she's completely stunned.

She sits herself up and opens her mouth, and I watch a myriad of emotions cross her features as she struggles to speak. She tries again, but this time it's nothing but her quickening breath turning into her gasping for air.

"Hey, Rain-e girl. Hey." I rush into the room and scoop her up in my arms as I sit on the edge of the bed. "I got you. Breathe in." I inhale loudly, hoping the feel of my chest rising and falling against her somehow helps calm her down. "Now breathe out. Can you do that again for me? In and out."

We inhale and exhale together until I feel the tension in

Raine's body slowly but surely loosen. I rub my hand up and down her back until I feel her shoulders shake in my hold.

"It's okay," I soothe. "Just let it all out."

My eyes sting and my chest aches at the sound and feel of her sobs, but I'm determined to be her solid ground right now. Her rock. Her shoulder. Her father.

I press my lips to her head as I slowly rock her in my arms. "I love you, Rain-e girl. I love you. I love you. I love you. I love you."

I catch movement in my periphery and see Zara standing in the doorway, bathrobe on, hair tied in her usual messy bun, and the sadness I feel in the marrow of my bones written all over her face. She places a palm over the center of her chest, and a single tear runs down her cheek. I feel her heart shatter for Raine, even more than I feel my own.

Zara closes the door, and I'm both humbled by the trust she has in me to comfort Raine and completely terrified at how ill equipped I really feel.

It takes another ten solid minutes for Raine's breathing to even out, and I'm convinced she's fallen asleep, completely depleted after all the tears, when her wet, croaky voice breaks the silence.

"What are you doing here?"

The question doesn't hold any accusation, but it's full of concern and curiosity. She pulls herself out of my hold and tilts her head up to look at me, her eyes red rimmed, swollen, and expectant. She wants answers.

"Are you okay?" I try to broach her outburst delicately, knowing my presence is the trigger and wanting so desperately to try and rectify that. "Do you want me to go get you a glass of water, maybe?"

"No." She shakes her head and climbs her way off her bed, wiping at her tear-streaked face and putting some distance between us. "I just want to know why you're here."

"I came to apologize," I admit. "I came to maybe talk about all the things I've done wrong by you since Lola died."

I catch the smallest flinch at the mention of her sister. "I didn't do right by you or your dad and your mom, and I'm trying to rectify that."

She remains silent as I speak, but she's back to sitting on the edge of the bed and I take her proximity to me as somewhat of a win.

"Did you know I asked your Dad for a divorce?" This probably isn't the best way to start this conversation, but honesty is the only tool in my arsenal right now.

Her eyes narrow, but she doesn't say anything, so I continue. "Your dad said that he would give me a divorce, but we had to go to therapy first. And I thought I had it in the bag," I admit to her. "We were going to see this therapist. I was going to show up a few times and then I would be able to say to him, 'I did it, now let me go.' It didn't go that way."

Trying to act nonchalant, I manage to kick my shoes off, and I scoot myself far enough up her bed that my back is resting on the headboard. "Turns out you learn a few things in therapy. One of those things is how badly I have let you down this last year." I can't hide the crack in my voice. "I have been very selfish. I have depended on your mom and dad to step up every time I failed, and that wasn't fair to them. And it was extremely unfair to you."

I pinch the bridge of my nose, trying to stave off the tears. "And I'm worried that I made you feel—" A sob escapes my throat. "Unloved and like you weren't enough. And I will never forgive myself for doing that to you."

I tilt my head back and release a shuddering breath, trying to get a handle on my emotions. I do not want to run the risk of Raine feeling like she needs to be the caretaker in this situation.

When I manage to drop my gaze back to her, her eyes are filled with unshed tears she's determined not to let fall.

She wipes her nose with the back of her hand. "Are you getting a divorce?"

It's not what I expect her to say, but I'll take any question if it means she's talking to me.

"I don't want to," I confess. "I haven't told your dad that yet, though. And truthfully, he might want one now, and I'll have to deal with that."

"Why do you think he'll want one?"

"Because sometimes we hurt the ones we love, and sorry just doesn't cut it."

"But did you apologize?"

I think back to us the other day, standing at Lola's grave. "I'm trying. I'm trying with all of you," I add. "I want to make things right. Especially with you."

"Do you love Lola more than me?"

Her question is a slap to the face. Her eyes bore into mine as she waits for my answer, and I am in awe of her courage and strength.

"Why do you think I love her more?" I ask.

"Because she's biologically yours," she says matter-of-factly. "And I'm not."

My chest cinches at her revelation. The realization that she and I are carrying around the exact same insecurity has me hating myself a little bit more for causing her that type of pain.

Of all the ways for us to be similar.

She doesn't know that Lola wasn't biologically mine. We didn't even think keeping this piece of information from everyone would matter.

"Rain-e girl," I breathe out. "None of that is true."

I swing my legs over the edge of the bed, rising and walking around to Raine. I drop to my knees in front of her and hold her hands in mine.

Inhaling loudly, I try to find the same courage and strength that exudes off of this beautiful, intelligent, young woman, and admit to her some of my deepest darkest secrets.

"After Lola died, I told myself that you and your mom and dad didn't need me. I convinced myself that because I wasn't biologically your dad, you didn't need me," I explain, every part of me heavy with shame. "I told myself your dad could live a wonderful life without me and without having to pick up all my messy pieces. I have spent more than a year telling myself that I was doing nothing more than weighing this family down. I believed if I stayed away you would all soon realize you were better off without me.

"But the problem with that is, it isn't the truth. For a while it was *my* truth, but there is actually nothing factual about the way I was feeling."

Raine's expressions change as she takes in my every word. I want to tell her that Lola wasn't biologically mine, but I want to try and make my point more.

"If I said to you, your life is better off without me because I'm not biologically your dad, what would you say to me?"

Raine tilts her head to the side as she contemplates my question. I'm surprised by the confidence I have in her answer. Surprised by the moment of clarity I have been blessed with at the hands of a seventeen-year-old.

"Papa, I would tell you you were wrong," she says, holding her hand out to me. I take it, squeezing it like a life raft. Taking the olive branch. "Life isn't better without you as my dad; life is better because of it."

CHAPTER TWENTY

NOW

I DON'T KNOW of any marriage that is perfect, but I feel like the life we lived before we lost Lola was damn near close.

I know for certain that there is a good chance we may never be that way again, but for the first time I don't feel anxious about what our future looks like.

After our impromptu visit to Lola's gravesite, and his talk with Raine, things between Leo and I have shifted—almost like we're both seeing the other in a different light.

Apart from the small, intimate funeral we had for Lola, Leo and I had never been to the cemetery together, a true sign that we both have been grieving apart and differently.

While that session with Dr. Sosa started out so heavy, visiting Lola and giving myself permission to let go and cry was painful and cathartic.

Having Leo there to catch me while I fell was everything I was too scared to admit I needed. It wasn't just about allowing myself to grieve, but it was about the man I married making me feel secure and safe.

I didn't know I needed that.

I'm the caretaker, the provider, and the protector. It's such an integral part of my personality, that it's hard to resolve with the instant relief I felt at being held and comforted.

It bridged a gap that only weeks ago I didn't know was possible. Our dynamics were forever changing, and this time it finally feels like it's a change for the better.

The weight on Leo's shoulders is visibly lifting, and his physical appearance is reaping all the benefits. I didn't realize how accustomed I'd become to the hunch in his shoulders, his tired eyes, and the gradual loss of weight and muscle.

Those things didn't make him any less beautiful, but they made his pain and baggage visible for all to see. But this version of him, with his hair cut, the color in his cheeks returning, and his body filling out; I'm turned on by the spark of hope in my husband alone.

"I love that you still swim."

Leo's voice pulls me out of my thoughts.

"Why's that?" I ask as I wade through the water to be closer to him.

"You swimming is the most consistent thing in our entire relationship, and I like knowing everything hasn't changed." I fold my arms on the edge of the pool as Leo sits down on the concrete patio, then unties his shoes and takes them off. His socks follow. "What's got you in the water today?"

Everything. Nothing. You.

"Nothing in particular," I lie. "I was able to finish up work early and had a few hours to kill before dinner. How was your day?"

The back and forth between us is new. It turns out, after a year or more of living in flight or fight, we forgot who we were before all the stilted conversations and silent treatments.

We found ourselves making more of a concerted effort to engage in small talk, to ask questions and listen to answers.

He averts his gaze as he plucks at the loose threads of his distressed jeans. "Today was good," he says. "I had lunch with one of the therapists from the rehab program and set up a plan for myself once the mandated sessions are over."

While we're in a positive and hopeful place overall, there are still so many little details we have yet to discuss; Leo's drinking is one of them.

I've noticed that he's stopped, or at the very least was choosing not to drink at home. I don't know if I was expecting extreme withdrawals or mood swings, but besides him no longer leaving the house and coming home drunk, there are no other obvious ways to acknowledge the change.

Feeling courageous, I ask him, "Are you still drinking?"

He finally raises his eyes to meet mine and shakes his head, and I feel the relief in my limbs, grateful that the water is carrying me.

"I'm not doing the whole alcoholics anonymous setup," he explains. "Where I count my alcohol-free days and celebrate those milestones."

Pushing myself off the edge of the pool, I back away from him. I point to the pile of my clothes that sit haphazardly next to our lounge chairs. "You could come in and explain it all to me."

It's a long shot, the man hates the cold more than anything else. And even though our pool is heated, Leo's version of heated is hot-tub hot.

But I want to be able to do this. For us to be able to tell each other the hard stuff without the distance we're so sadly used to.

I'm pleasantly surprised when he stands and starts taking his clothes off. When he reaches his underwear, he raises an eyebrow at me. "Are yours on or off?"

I don't bite back my response because it's been such a long time since I casually flirted with my husband.

"You've been around these parts long enough to know the answer to that."

If nobody else was home, they were always off.

He shucks them down his legs and I marvel at the naked man before me. Life had changed us, age had changed us, but the way his body calls to mine is a constant.

"Don't get any ideas," he playfully warns. "I still want to talk to you about how my day went."

I raise my hands in surrender. "I can keep them to myself, you know."

Leo offers me a knowing smirk as he slowly walks down the pool steps. He knows me well, and while there is no way I want to keep my hands to myself, if he needs me to, I can.

His teeth are clenched as he submerges himself neck-deep in the water. "Fuck, this was a terrible idea."

Chuckling, I swim toward him, holding out my hand for him to take.

When his palm sits on top of mine I wrap my fingers around his hand and pull him to me. His legs wrap around my waist and arms around my neck, the water the only thing able to get between us. I move us toward the nearest edge and plant a kiss below his ear. "Tell me what you want to tell me."

His body shudders at the sound of my voice and I feel mine already reacting to his presence.

He rests his head on my shoulder and I press soft kisses along his shoulder, just waiting for him to talk.

"I spent years not wanting to be my parents," he tells me. "And it kills me to know it was all for nothing. That even with all the times I chose to not drink and be sober, I still ended up here, like them."

I want to open my mouth to protest and tell him that his parents weren't dealing with the loss of their child, but I've learned enough to know that giving him excuses for his drinking isn't conducive to his healing. He needs to take responsibility for his actions and the consequences they incur.

Instead, I keep my mouth on his skin and one hand running up and down the length of his back, and the other hand holding him tightly to me, giving myself something to do while reminding him I'm still here, listening.

"In case it wasn't obvious," he continues, "I was drinking because I had no healthy ways to work through Lola's death." His voice cracks as he says her name. "Every time I felt something, I drank. Sad. *Drink*. Mad. *Drink*. Lost. *Drink*."

He lifts his gaze and meets my eyes. "Everything hurt, so I just drank." A humorless laugh leaves his mouth. "And do you know what the worst part is? I can't think back to a time where I can say with complete confidence that I drank and felt nothing. Numb? Yes. Did it dull the ache a little? Yes. But did it allow me to feel nothing? Not a single fucking time."

He seems furious with this revelation, and I make the conscious decision not to let him beat himself up. We can't change the past, and beating ourselves up over it doesn't help.

"Baby." I curl my hand around his neck. "When was your last drink?"

We both know I'm distracting him from focusing on all the ways he's failed, and I don't care. He is sitting in my arms, talking me through his decision to stop drinking and being committed to that decision, and there is no way I am going to let him focus on anything but that.

"The day I came to see you at work."

"Why that day?"

His hands cradle my jaw. "I hadn't drank since the night you came home from the bar."

I know which night he's referring to. "You knew I was at a bar?"

He scoffs. "Did you forget you had your tongue in my mouth a few hours later? I could taste the whisky every time you kissed me."

I shake my head shamefully. "I'm sorry about that night. The drinking and the way I—"

He slaps a hand across my mouth. "I don't want or need an apology. Not for any of it, but especially not *that*.

"That night I felt how much it hurt you to love me," he admits. "But I also felt just how much you did. I hated seeing you like that, but when I saw you at work, I realized just how close you were to giving up."

We haven't spoken about his request for a divorce, and no matter how right he feels in my arms, and just how good things are moving along, I need those words.

I need that one word.

Grabbing his wrist, I kiss the inside of his palm and drag his hand away from my mouth. "Do you still want a divorce?"

His thumb skims across my lips. "I can't believe I ever told you I wanted one."

"Do you still want a divorce?" I repeat.

"No," he breathes. "No. No. No."

My mouth finds solace in his, and like a freed hostage, my heart swells with relief. I want to believe our love is a great love, a true love, but unfortunately, the hard lesson to learn is that it doesn't actually matter which one of those it is. Because with great love comes great loss, and with true love comes true pain.

And no love is invincible.

His tongue sweeps through my mouth, and I feel the resounding beat of desire thrum between us.

"I told you not to get any ideas," he says in between kisses.

"Marry me."

I feel the stretch of his lips against mine and the rumble of a laugh deep in his chest. "Always."

CHAPTER TWENTY-ONE

NOW

IT'S THERAPY DAY.

I'm beginning to like therapy day.

When I demanded that Leo and I see Dr. Sosa, I had no expectations. I'd just grabbed on to her like a lifeline, hoping that even if he and I couldn't work it out, that at least she could try and get through to help him.

Now that we're coming out on the other side, I hate to think of where we would be without Dr. Sosa; as individuals and as husbands.

"Jesse," Dr. Sosa greets. "You're looking well today."

"I'm feeling well," I admit. "Leo's just on the phone, he'll be in in a second."

"I'm so glad you two are still choosing to continue with therapy," she praises. "Sometimes after such great major breakthroughs it's so easy to feel on top of the world and stop it completely."

Leo and I have spoken about continuing therapy. Individually, I know he is one hundred percent committed to the cause. Between his determination not to drink, and his dedication to his grief and loss journey, I couldn't be more proud. As a couple, neither of us think we need to come too often, but we agree that checking in every month with Dr. Sosa, for the time being, couldn't hurt.

"How's Raine?" she asks. "And Zara?"

Frequent therapy means your therapist knows your entire family by their first names. "They're good. The four of us seem to have found a nice balance of things."

"Sorry I'm late." Leo walks in and takes a seat beside me.

The man he was when we started and the man he is today, are night and day. And I'm falling more in love with the new version of my husband every damn day.

His thigh presses into mine, his hand resting on my knee, and I revel at the fact that only weeks ago, he and I would sit on opposite sides of the room.

"How're things going for you both?" Dr. Sosa asks, our check-in sessions much more laid back than they used to be.

"We're goo—"

"We're good," Leo says, interrupting me. "But there is something I want to talk about."

I feel myself frown, wondering why he didn't say anything beforehand.

He squeezes my knee, attempting to reassure me. "We have never broached the topic of having more kids."

My hand covers his, and on instinct we both shift on the couch to face one another.

His eyes are apprehensive when he starts talking. "I would be lying if I said it doesn't break my heart that I don't get to watch you be a father to another child of ours."

"Leo." I shake my head, needing him to hear this sooner

rather than later. "Baby, I know what you're going to say and I'm already with you."

"You are?" he asks incredulously.

"I don't want to risk putting us through anything like this ever again." I tap at my chest. "I can't do that again."

I watch his whole body exhale in relief. "Are you sure?" he asks again.

"Do you remember why we went with surrogacy?" I prompt. I don't wait for him to answer. "We got lucky. And I know how weird it sounds to say that, after everything we've been through, but it's true.

"We were so lucky to have Zara. She was able to donate her eggs, she agreed to be our surrogate, and we had sperm."

"Well..." hHe tries to interrupt.

"Okay, fine." I roll my eyes. "I had sperm. We didn't have to go through the process of finding someone or searching for egg donors or anything, really. It was within our reach, so we went with it."

"There are so many ways to have a family," I continue. "But for us, at the time, it was the most accessible option."

"And now, you're just okay with no more kids?" he asks.

"I'm okay with waiting and deciding how the next year is." I half stand off the couch before holding his hands and kneeling in front of him. "I'm okay with making my husband and his mental health a priority. I'm okay with making *my* mental health a priority. I'm okay with admitting defeat and saying that maybe some things aren't for us.

"And I'm okay with all of that, because now, after the year we've been through, I finally have all of you."

Doesn't he know how much I fear losing him?

"I just wanted to make sure," he confesses. "I wanted to give us the option to talk about it in a safe space if we needed to."

Leo and I both look at Dr. Sosa, who points to herself. "Hi. I'm the safe space."

I chuckle before looking back at him. "I'm sure. And if I change my mind on anything, I promise I'll let you know."

He grabs my face, bringing my lips to his. "I love you."

"I love you too," I say. "That'll always be the one thing that's never going to change."

"What's this?" I ask, walking into our candlelit house after returning from dropping Raine off at Zara's.

Leo meets me in the middle of the living room. Sliding his hands around my middle, I rest my own hands on his ass. "You're always doing stuff for me, and I wanted to do something for you."

"Something like…?" I smirk at him suggestively.

He chuckles. "Among other things. But did you want to eat first?"

I pretend to weigh it up with my hands. "Food or sex? Food or sex?"

He swats my chest. "I cooked your favorite. Let's eat it first."

"Hold up." I squeeze his ass cheeks to keep him in place. "You cooked mushroom risotto?"

"Is that so hard to believe?"

I pretend to avert my eyes.

"Okay, so it's taken me seven years, but I finally worked out the dumb rice and liquid consistency. Honestly, you could love any. Other. Meal."

I lower my mouth to his. "Thank you."

"For what?"

"For not giving up on the risotto." I tilt my head. "And us."

I attempt to kiss him, but he gives me his cheek. "I know what you're doing, Jesse. Get your mouth and your magic dick away from me. It's food time first."

Not even caring about the rejection, I kiss along his jawline instead. "Tell me more about my magic dick."

"You're relentless, you know that?" He faces me and bites my bottom lip. "Maybe I'll bend you over real good, help you work up an appetite."

My tongue sweeps over the sting of his teeth as I raise a brow at his choice of wording. "You'll bend me over?"

"I told you tonight was all about you."

Gently, I kiss the corner of his mouth. "If it's all about me, don't you think I deserve to know what you've got planned for me?"

"Please, Mr. Bottom from the Top, I ain't no rookie."

I rear my head back to meet his gaze. "Are you sure?"

I begin to take my clothes off, my t-shirt first and then my pants.

"What are you doing?" Leo asks.

"I want to be well prepared for whatever you have planned for me."

He tilts his head up to the sky, very much exasperated by my antics.

"So you're getting naked in the living room now?" he asks.

"Well, I just dropped Raine off, so I don't think she's making an appearance here any time soon." I push my boxers down my legs and enjoy the way Leo's eyes eat up every morsel of my exposed skin.

His gaze stalls at my cock, and I give it a little tug for good measure.

"Fuck me," he mutters under his breath.

I wink at him. "Gladly."

A timer goes off in the kitchen and Leo just looks at me and laughs. "This risotto is going to taste like clumps of glue and it's going to be all your fault."

"A for effort, though, right?"

He laughs. "Fuck you." He gestures to my naked body. "Don't fucking move. I'll be right back."

"Preferably with all your clothes off," I call out.

We used to do this all the time. Laugh and joke and antagonize one another during sex. Strangely, it was my favorite foreplay, the way we could go from fun to fucking in one single breath.

When Leo returns, he's naked, and now it's my turn to devour him with just one look. He's got a blanket and pillow in one hand and a tub of lube in the other.

"It's safe to say I don't think we're going to make it to the bedroom."

Stepping forward, I take the blanket and pillow out of his hands and spread them out across the carpet. He hands me the lube and I just toss it onto the blanket.

"I missed this," Leo says, reading my mind. "Just enjoying and existing in the moment instead of drowning in it."

I hold my hand out to him, and when he takes it, I tug him to me. We're standing chest to chest, completely naked, and for the first time in a very long time, with not a single care in the world.

"Sometimes I feel like there aren't enough letters in the alphabet to string the right words together to tell you how much I love you." He's not a man of many words, my Leo, but when he does make big declarations, he completely sweeps me off my feet.

"I love you, Jesse."

He coaxes us both to the floor as he slants his mouth over mine, repeating those treasured three words over and over with every move of his lips.

"Let me show you how much I love you," he whispers. "Make up for all the days I should've told you and I didn't."

"Leo." I try to protest, but he just guides my body back till I'm lying down, his mouth never leaving mine.

"Close your eyes, baby," he instructs. "Let me take care of you."

I allow myself to indulge in the sound of his voice and the way his lips move from my mouth to my body. He drops kisses down my neck, across my collarbone. He plays with my nipples. Tongue, fingers, and teeth.

"You're so beautiful," he whispers down my sternum, past my happy trail. He buries his face in my groin and my cock throbs at his proximity.

"Can I suck you off, baby?"

This was my favorite thing about when Leo took the reins. He still asked for permission as he took everything he wanted from my body.

I put my hand at the back of his head, guiding him to where we both want him to be. I feel his hot breath on my crown, followed by the tip of his tongue in my slit.

"Jesus fucking Christ," I groan.

He bobs up and down on my cock, getting deeper and sloppier, just the way I like it. He alternates between sucking my balls and keeping the tip of his finger pressed firmly right behind them.

"I don't want to come yet," I tell him, my voice hoarse and desperate. "I need you inside of me."

I tug at his hair in warning, needing him more than ever.

"Turn around," he instructs. "Let me see that beautiful ass of yours." Then he adds, "And put that pillow underneath you."

I do everything he asks, my body desperate to please him.

He spreads me wide and wastes no time, repeatedly swiping his tongue over my hole.

"Fuck, baby. You do that so good," I groan.

He spears my center with the tip of his tongue, teasing me, tasting me, getting me wet and ready for him.

I hear something drop beside me, and I turn my head to see the tub of lube.

"I want to see you get yourself ready for me," he demands. "How quickly you do it, how desperate you are for my cock."

Without hesitation, I coat two of my fingers and am surprised when Leo spreads my cheeks, giving me complete access to myself.

I moan as I thrust my fingers inside myself, rough and fast, wanting his cock more than

I need my next breath.

"Please, Leo," I beg. "Please fuck me."

He's squeezing the globes of my ass and keeping them spread as he guides himself inside me. I feel every ridge and pulse as he repeatedly thrusts. Hard and fast.

It's been such a long time since he's been inside me, but the way my body burns and stretches for him reminds me why I love it this way.

He is the only one I have ever wanted inside me. Me, like this, was only ever going to be for him.

"Jesus, Jesse," he grits out. "I love you so fucking much. This lifetime and the next and the one after that." He fucks me harder, hitting my prostate over and over again. "None of it will ever be enough."

His body hovers over mine, covering me as he continues to torture me deliciously.

Whatever frenzy he was feeling is lessening, his body moving slower, his thrusts deep but longer.

His mouth is right below my ear, whispering with every stroke.

I love you.

You were made for me.

Thank you for loving me.

Thank you for not leaving me.

I feel my body melting into a puddle of complete euphoria as every heartfelt word leaves his mouth.

This is us. Forever in love.

Perfectly imperfect.

We loved and we lost.

And we lost and we lived.

It's always going to be Jesse and Leo. No matter what life throws our way, you will always find us together.

Trying.

Fighting.

Loving.

"Leo," I cry out. "I'm going to come."

"Do it, baby. No hands. Come for me."

The tidal wave hits me without warning, cum spilling all over the blanket. My breath is ragged, my body twitching, as I feel Leo slip out and come all over my ass.

I'm shattered in the best possible way, on the floor of

the house I share with my husband, as he rubs his cum into my skin, marking me.

"Leo," I breathe out, the words just not enough.

He presses his lips to the middle of my shoulder. "I know, baby. I know."

This is it. This is life. And there isn't a single place I'd rather be.

CHAPTER TWENTY-TWO

NOW

LEO and I are lying on the couch together, arms and legs wrapped around one another, watching, but not really watching, some Netflix documentary about long-lost triplets in the background.

We do this a lot.

Not the documentary watching part, but the sitting and holding and touching. There is something extra special about being in one another's presence and having the freedom to kiss and talk with your loved one.

It's something people always say they took for granted when they specifically spoke about death. How heart-breaking it was to know it was the last time you said "I love you," or how you didn't know it was the last time you made love to your partner.

But nobody ever tells you about having those exact same moments when you're alive. How one moment you're laughing and the next your whole world burns to the ground around you.

I didn't know it would be almost a year before I would touch my husband again. I didn't know it would be a year without me telling him I loved him. A year without holding him, tasting him, *being* with him.

Nobody ever prepares you for that.

So now we love with purpose. When the cold and lonely nights come, because they will and they do, we are warmed by the memories of better times. Knowing that they exist and, just like the hard times, they will come back around too.

"Marry me," I whisper into his hair.

"We're already married, baby."

It's the same question with a new response. It's our latest tradition after our worst season.

My lips find their way to his neck and I move them up and down as I grind myself against him. His arm stretches back, his hand about to slip between my sweats and my underwear, when the front door swings open and Raine storms in with Zara hot on her heels.

"Okay, well that's not happening," Leo murmurs as he quickly reaches for a throw pillow to cover the tent in his pants. I jokingly press mine into his ass, letting him know I'm glad he's hiding my erection, and he grits out, "Stop it. Now."

It's been a long time since Zara and Raine felt comfortable enough to visit our house and come through our door unannounced. Despite their bad timing tonight, I will never not love the freedom they feel to come and go as they please.

Their presence here lately is our reminder that the heavy weight has lifted and our storm has finally rolled on through.

"Well, we're here," Zara says to Raine. "You may as well tell them both now since we're all together."

At this, Leo and I are no longer concerned with our missed orgasms, our attention solely focused on whatever it is that has Zara and Raine giving attitude to each other. We sit up properly on the couch just as Zara takes the single recliner and Raine sits on the carpet, cross-legged in the middle of the floor.

"I wasn't going to say anything just yet, but as you know, I submitted a few college applications. And Mom thinks I need to prepare you—"

"I did not use the word 'prepare,'" Zara interrupts. "I said it would be nice to give your fathers a heads-up that you may be leaving."

"Leaving?" I echo, just as Raine whines, "Mom."

"All my applications are for out-of-state universities."

"All of them?" Leo asks. "Nothing here in Seattle?"

I can't help but ask while my gaze flicks to Zara's, "Is this because of—"

"No," Raine answers firmly before looking straight at Leo. "This isn't because of Lola. Yes, I didn't get the chance to ease you all into the idea like I would've preferred because of everything that happened, but none of that is the reason I'm leaving Seattle."

"Okay. I want names of states and cities and each of the colleges," I say. "Only after thorough research has taken place will I allow you out of my sight."

I'm only half joking, but Raine doesn't seem to be pleased either way.

"I have applications in California, Washington, DC, Colorado, and Connecticut," she lists. "I applied for all queer-inclusive schools in the states with the most queer-friendly policies."

I want her close because she's my baby girl and after losing Lola, I wanted to put Raine in my pocket and keep her there for eternity. But how can I do that when her motivations are so altruistic?

She is going to change the world, and I get to have a front row seat while she does it. That's where my focus needs to be.

I feel Leo slide his hand into mine, squeezing, standing right by my side as we prepare for the next chapter of our lives together.

"I mean, it's not that big of a deal is it?" Leo pacifies. "There's social media and FaceTime, so it's not like we're not going to talk to each other every day. And I'm sure we can rack up those frequent-flyer miles if we all visit often."

"There's one condition, though," Raine says. "Mom has to come with me wherever I go."

The parent in me is thrilled for Zara to follow her. But the guy who's had the same best friend by his side for thirty odd years is shocked.

Zara offers me a sad smile from her seat opposite me. "I need a fresh start," she admits. "And we're all in a good enough place that I finally feel comfortable leaving."

I could read between the lines—it's her turn to find herself. And Leo and I owe her that.

"So, when do we find out where you got accepted?" Leo asks, steering the conversation.

"I should know in about three months."

"Okay, you know what that means." I jump out of my seat. "We're gonna need lists, itineraries, shared calendars, the whole lot."

Raine buries her head in her hands and groans, but I don't miss the spread of the smile stretched across her face through all the fingers.

"Speaking of good news," Leo says, "I have some too."

I rack my brain, trying to figure out if I missed something he may have said in the last couple of days, but I come up empty.

"I got a job at Duquette's," he announces, his eyes on a knowing Raine.

I know returning to the workforce is a big deal for Leo, but I haven't pressured him, hoping he knows there's no rush. Money would come and go, but there is no price on his mental health.

"How come I didn't know about this?" I glare at Raine. "Why do you know this?" Then it hits me and I turn my head to look at him. "Did you know about the out-of-state college applications?"

"What?" He shrugs innocently. "We tell each other stuff."

Pretending to be put out, I glance back at Raine, even though internally I love that they now "tell each other stuff." "So, tell me about your Dad's new job."

He playfully nudges me on the shoulder and I put my arm around him, kissing his temple.

"Well, you know how your receptionist, Demi, moved to Colorado," Raine explains. "Deacon asked if Pa wanted to replace her."

"Well, it didn't go exactly like that." Leo expands on Raine's brief explanation. "When I visited you that time, I noticed Demi had left but didn't really think twice about it. And then when he and I spoke last week, I asked if he had filled the role and if he hadn't, that I was interested."

"Are you working every day?"

He nods. "Same schedule as you. Five days a week and every second Saturday."

"We could totally carpool," I add.

Leo leans in and kisses me. "Baby, you say the sexiest things."

"Well, that's my cue to go to my room," Raine says, picking herself up off the floor. "That's already one bad joke too many."

"But I've got so many more," Leo calls at her retreating back.

"Thanks, but no thanks."

The three of us laugh in unison, and I could cry from the sound. It feels so good to joke, albeit at Raine's expense, but to joke nonetheless.

"I also told Deacon that my therapy sessions are non-negotiable for me and I would need to work my appointments into my schedule." Leo's eyes dart between Zara and me. "I'm telling you both because I want to be kept accountable. I want to be called up on my shit if things happen to change or decline."

I want to tell him not to be too hard on himself, but this full-throttle approach is what he chose for himself, and I need to respect that.

"I can't imagine that was easy to do," Zara acknowledges. "I'm so proud of you for putting your mental health first and being upfront when you needed to be."

"I couldn't have done any of this without the three of you." Leo turns to me. "Your patience and persistence to never give up on me."

I place a hand on his back and rub up and down soothingly. He accepted his need to heal and is committed to his growth, but he often forgets that none of us had truly dealt with Lola's death, and a lot of our own coping mechanisms were just as unhealthy as his.

There's a knock on the door that interrupts our conversation and I remember that Julian and Deacon were stopping by tonight.

"Come in," I call out, heading to meet them at the front door.

Zara looks toward the door. "Shit. Raine and I should've called before coming over."

I shake my head at her. "Don't be silly. This is your house too. And it's Julian and Deacon."

She glances around the room. "You know what? I'm going to pass. I'll see if Raine wants to come with me or stay. And if she stays, I'm going to go out."

I smirk at her knowingly. "Is that what we're calling it these days?"

"Shut up," she retorts.

I open the door to find Julian and Deacon kissing on my front patio and I hear Zara say, "Yeah, I'm getting out of here. The color green does not look good on me."

"Sorry to interrupt, love birds, but would you like to come inside? Because I can close the door until you're ready."

Laughing, they pull away from one another. "We would love to come inside," Julian says.

I open the door wider and both men walk in just as Zara gets ready to walk out.

"Raine staying?" I ask her.

"Yes."

I crane my neck and kiss her on the top of her head. "Have fun *going out*," I tease.

She flips me off as she retreats to her car. "Fuck off. I love you."

"RAIN-E," I PUSH HER BEDROOM DOOR OPEN AND SHE GLANCES UP at me from the book she's reading.

"Stop trying to make Rain-e happen, Dad. I told you only Papa calls me that."

"Sorry." I put my hands up in surrender and take a seat on the edge of her bed. "Can I talk to you for a second?"

She puts her book down. "Is everything okay?"

"You know how Papa and I see Dr. Sosa?" She nods. "Recently, we discussed Lola's nursery."

Raine's throat bobs and I know she, too, is remembering the day Zara was rushed to the hospital.

One moment we were setting up the nursery, and the next we were literally closing the door on a part of our lives that was too hard to handle.

The door has stayed closed.

It's still closed.

"Dr. Sosa suggested having people who didn't have the same emotional attachment to Lola to help us repaint the room."

She anxiously bites at her bottom lip. "So, they'll paint Lola's room?"

"Yes. And you're more than welcome to help them if you feel up to it," I explain. "But for Papa and me, it's something we don't think we can do."

She tugs at the skin on her lip, thinking about the offer. "Are they doing it tonight?"

"We didn't plan on it because I wanted to talk to you first."

"I want to help them," she blurts out. "Does Mom know?"

"She does," I assure her. "But she doesn't want to be here when they're painting."

"When will they do it?"

Apparently, I'm talking too slowly, because Raine pulls off her blankets and makes a beeline for Deacon and Julian.

"Can we paint the room tonight?"

"Raine," I warn, but she ignores me.

"Walmart is open; we can go and buy paint."

"Raine," I repeat, but Deacon shakes his head at me.

"We can do it tonight. We'll go pick out whatever colors you want and we'll stop at our place to pick up some clothes we can paint in and we'll be all set."

"Deac, I..."

The words don't come. The gratitude. The grief. The love. It's all just so much.

Acknowledging my loss for words, Deacon offers me a sympathetic smile. "We told you we wanted to do this for you and your family." He looks at his husband. "Julian can stay and start packing up the room. And if you're okay with it, Raine and I will go get paint."

I nod, more than okay with it. I shift my gaze to Leo, who's looking at Raine in awe.

I know the feeling. Our daughter is a force to be reckoned with, and her resilience is inspiring.

"Okay." Raine impatiently bounces on the balls of her feet. "Let's go. Let's go."

"Okay," I manage to say with a chuckle, Raine's enthusiasm is the levity both Leo and I need. "Go get my credit card out of my wallet and buy us some paint."

DR. SOSA HAD STRESSED THE IMPORTANCE OF COMING UP WITH A plan before asking someone else to pack up and paint Lola's room. The idea was to find people you respect and trust to do the emotional labor for you, without also impacting their own emotional state.

I hadn't thought of asking Deacon, but when I'd shared

with him what we were discussing in therapy, he offered that he and Julian could help us take that difficult step. Once that offer was on the table, Leo and I found it difficult to refuse.

With that, we explained to Julian and Deacon that everything in Lola's room was brand new. The excitement of a new baby had us buying things like crazy, which meant the untouched room was currently a small baby boutique on steroids.

It's hard knowing Julian is in there, let alone imagining him packing up all of her things. But the room is nothing but heavy heartache, and Lola deserved to be remembered with love and tenderness.

"Are you okay?" I ask Leo as I chop up a salad, just to give my hands something to do.

He's sitting on the kitchen counter. "It's such a weird feeling to want to help him but also accept that I can't do it."

"That's therapy, baby."

His sad chuckle mirrors my own.

"I know we're doing the right thing," I assure him. "For her memory and for ours."

"I hate that Zara isn't here," he muses.

I do too, but Zara recently sat us down for an extremely tough conversation, where she gently reminded us that she wasn't Lola's mother the same way she is Raine's. So asking for her permission or inclusion on things to do with Lola's belongings and her memories was appreciated but not necessary.

Truth be told, I know my best friend well enough to know that now that Leo and I were in a good place, she was trying to absolve our responsibility to her and her own grief.

But family doesn't work that way.

Our family doesn't work that way.

"I know Raine will take pictures for her anyway," I tell him.

"We're back," Raine calls out, interrupting us.

"Speak of the devil." Leo hops off the counter. "Hey, Rain-e girl. What you got?"

I look up at Deacon from my mess of vegetables. "How was it?"

"Perfectly fine," he answers with a smile. "Is Julian in the room?"

Leo and I nod as he points at Raine. "Come in whenever you're ready. I'll start taping the walls and floor."

Deacon heads over to Lola's room to join Julian while Raine sorts through a whole bunch of paraphernalia that has nothing to do with paint.

"Did you buy all of Walmart?" I ask her.

"Did you know you need to tape the walls when you paint?"

"Good deflection," I say.

She lifts her shoulders to her ears and smiles. "You'll miss me when I'm in a different state for college."

"No shame," I hear Leo murmur. "Girl has no shame."

RAINE: WE'RE READY.

HOURS HAD PASSED SINCE WE LEFT THE HOUSE, NOT WANTING TO be waiting around idly while they packed and painted the room. Since Zara ended up going out, Leo and I ended up watching television and talking together at her place while we waited to receive that text from Raine.

Now we're driving the short distance to our place and the nerves are settling in.

There isn't any real expectation on what it would look like, but trying to anticipate our reaction to the door being opened takes quite a large amount of mental energy.

Parking in the driveway, I'm not surprised that neither Leo nor I can manage to open our doors.

"We can do this," I coax.

"Can we?" Leo says. "Because it kind of feels like we can't."

I grab his hand and thread my fingers through his. "I love you, Leo."

"I love you too," he replies, raising our hands to his lips to kiss.

"Highs and lows," I say.

"Highs and lows."

I open my door first and then Leo follows. When we enter the house, Julian is stacking boxes in the living room. They're all labeled and positioned according to sizing.

It's less of a punch to the gut than I thought, but knowing what Leo and I have planned to do with all her things comforts me in more ways than one.

Julian looks up at the door as we walk in. "Hey. Deacon and Raine are just adding some final touches. Let me tell them you're here."

"Julian," Leo calls out, and Julian glances over his shoulder. "Thank you."

"Of course."

Leo slides his hands around my middle just as Raine walks out of the room and toward us. Her hair is sitting on top of her head and she's got paint streaks everywhere.

"Have a good time?" I ask.

The size of the smile transforms her face, but neither Leo nor I miss the unshed tears pooling in her eyes.

"Raine, babe." Leo drops his hands and she comes running into my arms.

"I just hope she likes it," she croaks out. "I didn't get to be a big sister, so I really hope she likes it."

"Of course she will," Leo says, wrapping his arms around us.

"Oh shit, sorry." Deacon's voice cuts through our moment. "We were just going to leave. We figured we would give you some privacy."

"Wait," I say. I kiss Raine on the top of her head. "Gimme a sec, babe." I turn to Deacon. "Leo and I wanted to talk to you about something."

I usher all of us to the living room, but Deacon declines sitting down so as not to get paint on the couch. So I stay standing, while Leo, Julian, and Raine sit.

I clear my throat. "Leo and I were discussing Lola's things. Everything is brand new and gender neutral." I glance at Raine. "Thanks to our daughter. And..."

The words get lodged in my throat. And my tongue refuses to work. I feel Leo's hand slide into mine, squeezing it.

"We would love for you two to have all of it," Leo says, his voice thick with emotion. "You're on your own surrogacy journey and we cannot wait for you two to welcome a brand new baby into your family."

Managing to compose myself, I add, "You both have done so much for us, and it would mean the world to know things we didn't get to use for our baby girl will go to another baby who will be so loved."

"Jesse," Deacon says, on an exhale. "Man, I can't..." He

looks between the three of us and then back at Julian, whose tears freely run down his face. "Thank you."

Deacon leans in for a hug and I take in a lungful of air as I hug him back. It feels like a brand new day.

The four of us hug and cry and say all our thank yous and goodbyes, and soon enough it's just Leo and me following Raine into Lola's room.

"Okay," she says, standing in front of the closed door. "You both have to close your eyes. Dad, hold Pa's hand and follow us in. Don't open your eyes until I say so."

She guides Leo in and I keep my hold on him and follow. I smell the paint and feel the freshness in the air even before I open my eyes.

My heart beats frantically inside my chest, knowing that a fresh coat of paint isn't going to take all our pain away, but we are a family that's healing, and healing also means honoring and remembering.

"Okay," Raine says. "Open your eyes."

I don't.

I keep them closed for a little while longer, hearing Leo's gasp for air followed by his praise for Raine.

"This is so perfect." A wet laugh leaves his mouth. "Gosh, how many more tears are there?"

"But they're happy ones, right?" Raine asks.

He must nod because silence falls across the room.

"Dad." Raine's voice is close, almost a whisper. "You can open your eyes now."

She slips her hand in mine, just as I feel Leo stand behind me. Opening my eyes, I feel the tears fall before my eyes can truly see what's in front of me.

"Let me give you both a tour," she says, standing between Leo and me, holding both our hands.

The room is painted in the original custard yellow color that Raine had picked the first time around, and she and Julian must've decided to keep the chest of drawers that sits beautifully against the back wall. It feels complete but not barren.

"I wrote on each wall in my own handwriting," Raine explains. "I hope you don't mind."

My eyes catch the first bundle of lines.

I told Pa and Dad I was leaving Seattle for college.

My fingers run over the black ink. "What's this?"

"They're just things I want to tell her." She points at another few lines and reads them out.

"I haven't told them yet that I got early admission into UCLA and I'm moving to Los Angeles."

"Raine," Leo scolds. "You're going to give your father a heart attack tonight."

She is. Thankfully, I'm too engrossed in her little wall of confessions to deal with it right now.

"So, what? You just wrote all your secrets on the wall?" I ask her.

"Yes and no," she replies. "I wrote down all the things I've been meaning to tell her. Just because she's not here doesn't mean I can't talk to her and share my life with her. She's my sister."

She drags Leo and me to the wall on the opposite side of the room. "These are a little bit different. Maybe a bit too sad for you and Pa."

I love that she is protective of our feelings, but I read the wall anyway.

Missed you today.

Wondered what color your hair would be.

I swipe at my tears. "This is a beautiful idea, babe."

"Here." She hands us each a marker. "You both can do it

too. Any time you think of something you want to tell her, just write it down."

I am in awe that our seventeen-year-old daughter eased our grief with innocence and resilience neither Leo nor I possess. She has thoughtfully given us a way to keep Lola in our memory, always.

"There's one more thing." She grabs a bag from the corner and pulls out what look to be photo frames. Raine walks over to the chest of drawers and lines each of them up beside one another. "Remember these?" she asks.

Leo and I had framed photos of all of us to keep in Lola's room. There was one of each of us from our wedding day, but next to it is the same looking frame, only it's a picture of our sleeping baby Lola.

"Jesse," Leo cries. He picks up the frame as I come up behind him, resting my hands on his shoulders. "She's so beautiful," he says through tears.

"Turn it around," Raine says.

I glance up at her. "What?"

"The picture frame," she reiterates. "Turn it around."

Leo does as she says. And there's a folded note. He opens it, but I'm the one who reads it out loud.

Dear Jesse and Leo,

My two very favorite men. Fathers to the two best girls.

I know it's been hard, and if I could've taken away all your pain in the last sixteen months, I would've done it in a heartbeat. The road to right now has been the hardest road any of us have traveled.

But your love prevailed.

I hope I find a love like yours.

I knew you would make it here one day, and I have been saving this photo till I knew you were both ready to see it.

Be kind to yourselves, give yourselves grace when you need it, and be proud of the men you are.

I love you both.

Xx

Zara

LEO

TWO YEARS LATER

"WE SHOULD'VE STOPPED her from going to college in another state," Jesse says as he grabs our overhead luggage, waiting to disembark the plane. "I hate being so far away from her."

"I did suggest moving to L.A.," I remind him.

"Zara's already there with her." He sighs. "And I don't want to smother her."

"Because the back and forth every six weeks and the five to six FaceTime calls a week aren't doing that," I murmur under my breath.

"I heard you." He nudges me. "And why are you so okay about it? I know you miss her."

"Of course I miss her, but this is where she wants to be. She's nineteen now." I rest my hand on the small of his back. "Zara being here with her should be a comfort for you."

"I just miss them both," he grumbles. "I didn't think we would ever live apart or even leave Seattle."

Raine and I had developed a new relationship in the last two years. And it was very different to the one she had with both Zara and Jesse. I was still her parent, she still called me Pa, and I loved her more than I ever thought was humanly possible. But Lola's death had shaped us. It had left some scars and we would forever be healing.

The most beautiful thing about our relationship is that we healed together.

Just like Jesse and I did, Raine and I went to therapy together. It was strange at first, because the power dynamic in our relationship wasn't the same. I was her father, I was the one who needed to be held accountable. I was the one who needed to prove his love for her while giving myself the grace to understand that I could be a present and attentive father and still be a man who was in mourning.

With Dr. Sosa's help, Raine was given a safe space to explore how much Lola's conception and stillbirth affected her as a sibling as well as a daughter. She was also encouraged to tell me how much I hurt her. I didn't want to leave any stone unturned. I didn't want to risk resentment. I wanted my daughter to know that no matter what she said or thought or felt about me, I wasn't going anywhere. I wasn't going to love her any less.

Raine was too much like Jesse, and he and I both wanted to make sure she knew she never needed to sacrifice her feelings, happy or sad, to save someone else's.

It was these things we'd learned together that allowed me to be completely comfortable with her going to college away from home in a way that Jesse wasn't.

His worries stemmed from not being one call away if she needed us. It didn't matter that Zara was in the same city, his control had no boundaries and wasn't driven by rhyme or reason.

Turning my cell off airplane mode, a message from Raine in our group chat pops up.

WAITING FOR YOU AT BAGGAGE CLAIM.

"She's here," I tell Jesse.

He grunts as the people in front of us start moving, and I don't even bother stifling my chuckle. The man goes from thirty-five to sixty-five whenever we fly to visit Raine. His impatience to see her makes him incorrigible.

It takes another ten minutes to make it to baggage claim, where Raine, her hair tinged gold from the sun, her skin completely tanned, looks so happy and content. Next to her is a smitten Zara and her girlfriend Clem, and Raine is holding a big sign that says "Marry Me."

Because there is only one person responsible for this fuck-off sign, I stop and turn, biting my bottom lip to try and hide my smile and look at the smiling fool that is my husband. "I don't know how many times I have to remind you we're already married."

He releases his hold on his hand luggage and tugs me closer to him, our arms wrapping around one another in the middle of the busy airport. "It doesn't hurt if you tell me again."

It blows my mind how far Jesse and I have come. How close I was to losing it all. There are still days, or even weeks, where the struggle to put one foot in front of the other is so real and reminding myself of the support system I have at my disposal is imperative. Because this life with this man is all I'll ever want.

If the great loss that he and I have survived has taught us anything, it's that we're not invincible. Neither is our marriage and neither is our love. Bad things absolutely happen to good people, but so do good things. And the former should never be given the power to eliminate the latter.

Fight for the good. Earn your right to deserve the good. Nurture and love the good. And let it matter less what we broke, than the fact that we found our way back to each other.

I bury my head in the crook of his neck and say the words he loves to hear. "I, Leo Ricci-Hunt"—I feel his pulse quicken against my lips—"take you, Jesse Ricci-Hunt, to be my husband, to have and to hold, from this day forward, for better, for worse, for richer, for poorer, in sickness and in health, to love and cherish, till death do us part."

Jesse sends the words into the air. Like a prayer. Like a promise. "I, Jesse Ricci-Hunt, take you, Leonardo Ricci-Hunt, to be my husband, to have and to hold, from this day forward, for better, for worse, for richer, for poorer, in sickness and in health, to love and cherish, till death do us part."

***

Did you enjoy What We Broke?

If you want to see more of Jesse and Leo, visit the link and sign up to my newsletter to receive an exclusive BONUS scene straight to your kindle.

http://www.marleyvbooks.com/bonus-epilogues-mv/

***

If you want to read Deacon and Julian's book, Without

You it is available on e-book, paperback and FREE with Kindle Unlimited

---

Want more MM Romance from Marley Valentine?

Unwanted: A Second Chance Romance
Ache: A Friends to Lovers Romance
<u>Devilry: A Teacher/Student Romance</u>
<u>Unforgettable (Vino & Veritas)</u>

**Tragedy brought us together, but something stronger made me
want to stay.**

Julian was the boy next door. My brother's best friend, he fit with my
family in ways I never could. While he and Rhett went on to play house, I
left the only life I knew, desperate for a fresh start.

Until everything changed.

Heartache came along, and the aftermath of my brother's death was here
to stay. I was now face to face with Julian more than I ever wanted to be.

Being around him brought up all my insecurities, forced me to deal with
hard truths, and conjured up feelings I had no business entertaining. He
wasn't the man I thought I knew. He was complex and layered, and
inherently beautiful in all the ways I'd never noticed.

Not on another person.

Not on another man.

Not until him.

PURCHASE WITHOUT YOU: A BROTHER'S BEST FRIEND ROMANCE

I couldn't tell you when I fell in love with Gael Herrera, but I wish I knew how to make it stop.

Falling in love with a straight man is a rookie mistake. But falling in love with my soon-to-be-married-to-a-woman best friend is nothing but heartache.

Through all the years, and all the men I've fooled around with, he's always been at the back of my mind. An unrequited crush I wish I could shake. A dream that was never going to come true.

When I whisk him off to a surprise bachelor party weekend in Vegas, I surrender to the idea that this is an opportunity for me to finally let go of my feelings for him and say goodbye.

But after a heated exchange and an even hotter kiss, everything I thought I knew about our friendship changed.

Maybe I had it wrong. Maybe, after all this time, we were more than best friends. Maybe, just maybe, he felt it too.

PURCHASE ACHE: A FRIENDS TO LOVERS ROMANCE

Two halves of a whole, Arlo Bishop and I were both
unwanted kids brought together by the foster system.
Dealing with the aftermath of neglect and abandonment,
we grew up side by side and found solace in one another.

We wanted.

We needed.

We loved.

Desperately.

But somewhere along the way, Arlo wanted and needed
and loved drugs more. So, I did the only thing I could and
broke my own heart to save his.

Now, four years later, I'm back in L.A. and face-to-face with
my past. Not only does the pain and hurt of our mistakes
linger between us, but so do our feelings.

I didn't plan on a second chance, fear of history repeating
itself making it hard to forgive and even harder to forget.

But with only one touch, one kiss, I was taken back to
where it all started.

Two halves of a whole, Arlo Bishop and I were made for for
each other. But we were no longer the unwanted foster
kids.

We were grown men.

And I wanted nothing more than him.

PURCHASE UNWANTED: A SECOND CHANCE ROMANCE

Attending King University was at the top of my bucket list. Falling in love with my professor wasn't.

Earning a full scholarship to King University was my hard earned ticket out of hell. I'm happy to be away from the small town I grew up in and all the equally small minded people who live there.

King was going to be my safe haven. A place where I could leave the old me behind and finally grow into the young man my family had desperately tried to hide away.

Diving head first into new experiences, new friends, and parties, I didn't expect to run straight into the one thing I wasn't ready for.

His arms are welcoming, his body is addictive and his lips are heaven. Cole Huxley is everything I could fall in love with, except for one problem... I never wanted to fall for my professor.

PURCHASE DEVILRY: A TEACHER/STUDENT ROMANCE

One night with Reeve Hale wasn't enough. I knew it when I kissed him, I knew it when I slept with him, and I was certain of it when I walked out of his motel room the very next day.

So when the shy, gorgeous man is introduced as our newest employee at Vino and Veritas, I can't help but conjure up all the ridiculous ways to convince him to repeat that unforgettable night. Like asking him to be my fake boyfriend at my sister's upcoming wedding.
Only, I didn't expect him to say yes.

Playing pretend shouldn't feel this real. Especially when Reeve is planning on leaving Vermont after the summer.

We agreed to one night. We negotiated a fake relationship. But I'm the one who broke our terms. I wasn't supposed to fall in love and he was never supposed to be so unforgettable.

PURCHASE UNFORGETTABLE: A WORK PLACE/ FAKE RELATIONSHIP ROMANCE

acknowledgments

Wow!
I can't believe I made it to the acknowledgements. For a second there I thought I was never going to finish this book. I mean, you know how it is. You start with a plan and then it all goes to shit, am I right?

For those of you who don't know, 9 weeks ago I gave birth to a beautiful baby boy. And while he was planned and came right on time, the plan to have my book finished before his arrival was less than successful.

To everyone who called me crazy for finishing this book with a newborn, you were right. To everyone who helped me regardless, I love you.

To my husband and my gorgeous children. Thank you for completing my world.

To my mother and sister who turned their whole lives upside down so I can finish this book. I am forever indebted to you.

Jodi, Laura and Kacey; my round the clock support system. I want to promise that I'll never do something this insane again, but I don't make promises I can't keep. Thank you for cheering me on right to the very last second and never losing faith in me. I love you all.

My Sipho! Another cover, another winner. I can't wait for everyone to see the next in the series.

To Marley's Mofo's, My ARC Team and all the Bloggers, You are the BEST readers a girl could ask for. Thank you for all your encouragement and support. For always showing up and sharing your love for my books. And especially for keeping up the hype for this book when all I wanted to do was let it burn.
I hope it delivered.

To my wonderful team, Jodi, Laura, Kacey, Layla, Shauna and ellie. Thank you for making my book the best it can be.

To Nikki and Teralynn for your assistance with Lennox's character.

To Kate Stewart, Joe Arden and Maxine Mitchell. I told myself I was allowed to relisten to The Ravenhood Trilogy when I finished my book. Thank you for being my motivation.

And last but never least, thank YOU, for picking this book up, reading my stories, loving them, or even hating them.

Until next time.
Much Peace and Love.

about the author

Marley Valentine

Living in Sydney, Australia with her family, Marley Valentine is a USA Today bestselling author and a former social worker who uses her past experiences to write real life, emotional and heartfelt contemporary romance.

She enjoys mixing it up with all types of romance pairings, incorporating all forms of life, lust and love as her characters embark on their journey to their happily ever after.

When she's not busy writing her own stories, she spends most of her time immersed in the words of her favourite authors.

Marley enjoys interacting with her readers so please feel free to reach out to her via Facebook, Instagram, email and/or subscribe to her newsletter.

Other Books by Marley Valentine

Light My Way | Find My Way | Reclaim | Revive | Rectify

MM Romance Books

Devilry | Without You | Ache | Unforgettable | What We Broke

The Unlucky Ones
Unwanted | Unloved | Unlikely

Find Marley

Facebook | Facebook Reader Group | Amazon Author Page | Goodreads Author Page | Twitter | Instagram | Website | BookBub | Newsletter